HUSKY with a HEART

by Ben M. Baglio

Illustrations by Ann Baum

Cover illustration by Mary Ann Lasher

AN
APPLE
PAPERBACK

SCHOLASTIC INC.

New York Toronto London Auckland Sydney
Mexico City New Delhi Hong Kong Buenos Aires

Special thanks to Andrea Abbott

No part of this publication may be reproduced, stored in
a retrieval system, or transmitted in any form or by any means, electronic,
mechanical, photocopying, recording, or otherwise, without written
permission of the publisher. For information regarding permission,
write to Working Partners Limited, 1 Albion Place, London W6 0QT,
United Kingdom.

ISBN 0-439-77523-X

Text copyright © 2005 by Working Partners Limited.
Created by Working Partners Limited, London W6 0QT.
Illustrations copyright © 2005 by Ann Baum.

All rights reserved. Published by Scholastic Inc., 557 Broadway, New York,
NY 10012, by arrangement with Working Partners Limited. ANIMAL ARK is a
trademark of Working Partners Limited. SCHOLASTIC, APPLE PAPERBACKS, and
associated logos are trademarks and/or registered trademarks of Scholastic Inc.

12 11 10 9 8 7 6   6 7 8 9 10 11/0

Printed in the U.S.A.   40
First Scholastic printing, January 2006

The Black Tor Huskies

Huskies that Mandy meets are indicated in **bold**.
In the pairings, the sire (father) is listed first.

Family One
War + Aurora = Bullet
Bullet + Helgi = **Havoc**, Crystal
Havoc + Ashia = **Freya**, **Malik**, **Bayonet**

Family Two
Sigurd + Snowflake = **Opal**, **Odin**, Copper
Havoc + **Opal** = **Robin**, **Keira**

Family Three
Cossack + Crystal = **Indy**
Copper + **Indy** = **Cindy**, **Orca**

Family Four
Thor + Crystal = **Dart**, **Galileo**, **Dakota**

Family Five
Thor + Willow = **Quiver**, **Alaska**
Malik + **Quiver** = **Aspen**, **Caspian**, **Vali**,
   Phantom, **Nemo**

One

Mandy Hope charged downstairs in the dark. In the hall, the phone jangled loudly, shattering the silence of the night. Upstairs, a door opened and Mandy realized her mom and dad must have woken up, too.

She ran into the hall and switched on the light. The clock on the wall showed it was close to four in the morning. She picked up the phone, knowing that a call to the Animal Ark veterinary clinic at this hour could mean only one thing: an emergency!

"Animal Ark," she said breathlessly.

"This is Hannah Burgess," said the voice at the other end of the line.

Mandy didn't recognize the name even though she knew practically everyone in Welford, the Yorkshire village where she lived.

"Sorry to call so early," Hannah continued as Mandy tried to guess from her tone how bad the news would be. The woman definitely sounded anxious, and when she paused to ask someone in the background if there was "any sign yet," Mandy gulped. Any sign of what? Of breathing? Of life?

"It's my dog Quiver," Hannah said to Mandy. "She's having puppies."

Just then, Dr. Emily Hope appeared in the hall and looked quizzically at Mandy. "What's up?" she asked.

Mandy signaled to her mom to wait a moment while Hannah finished talking.

"So far, everything looks fine," she said. "But it's Quiver's first litter, and I really would like a vet to be here. Would you mind coming out?"

Mandy was determined to be a vet one day, and she already knew a lot about animals from helping out in her parents' busy clinic. But not enough to make house calls yet. "It's my mom you want. She's right here." Mandy handed the receiver to her mom. "It's a lady named Hannah Burgess. Her dog Quiver is having her pups."

"Oh, right," said Dr. Emily, as if she'd been expecting the call. "Hannah breeds Siberian huskies. She came in the other day to register Quiver." She took the receiver and had a short conversation with Hannah, promising that either she or Dr. Adam Hope, Mandy's dad, would come out right away.

She hung up at the same time that Dr. Adam appeared in the hall, warmly dressed and carrying his vet's bag. "Where am I going, then?" He grinned. Clearly, he'd overheard the end of the conversation.

"There's a litter of puppies on the way," Mandy told him.

"At Black Tor Cottage," put in Dr. Emily.

"That's up near Mr. Matthews's place, isn't it?" asked Dr. Adam, taking the Land Rover keys off a hook on the wall.

Mr. Matthews, a dairy farmer, lived at Burnside Farm about five miles from Animal Ark.

"Right," said Dr. Emily. "Are you OK to go on your own?"

"Absolutely not," said Dr. Adam. He looked at Mandy. "I need my right-hand — uh, woman. You coming?"

"You bet!" Mandy was just about to head for the door when she realized she was still in her pajamas. "Just a minute, Dad! I need to change."

"Make it quick," said Dr. Adam.

In less than five minutes, she and her dad were on their way, driving past frost-covered fields on their way to Black Tor Cottage.

A tall, blond young man met them at the door. "I'm Hannah's fiancé, Michael Temperley," he greeted them. "Your timing's perfect. The first pup has just arrived. Hannah's with him and Quiver in the puppy room."

He took Mandy and her dad to a cozy room. A petite young woman with long, dark hair was kneeling next to a wooden box with three high sides and one lower side. It was lined with a fleecy blanket under several layers of newspaper. A light gray, blue-eyed husky lay on her side in the box, panting.

"Thanks for coming so quickly," said Hannah, looking up at Mandy and Dr. Adam.

"It's no trouble," Dr. Adam assured her after he'd introduced himself and Mandy. "How are you doing, Quiver?" he murmured, kneeling down beside the box. He smiled at Hannah. "This is a great whelping box. You're obviously well prepared."

Hannah smiled back. "Well, we've had quite a few litters, even though this is Quiver's first time."

Mandy crouched down next to her dad and caught her first glimpse of the puppy. Michael wasn't exaggerating when he said it had just arrived! Quiver was looking at him with surprise, her forehead wrinkled in a frown.

Michael bent down and smoothed Quiver's head. "It's all right, girl. That's your son."

But Quiver just stared at the slippery little parcel lying next to her.

"Come on, Quiver. Your baby needs you," Mandy said.

Tentatively, Quiver stretched toward the puppy and sniffed him. With a quick glance at her owners, she began to lick her new pup caringly, cleaning him up for his first day of life.

"Good girl," murmured Hannah, sounding very relieved.

As the puppy dried under his mother's energetic pink tongue, Mandy admired the dusky gray color of his fur. "He's just like his mom," she observed. She longed to cuddle the brand-new husky, but she knew better than to touch him so soon. Quiver wouldn't want to share him with anyone just yet.

Quiver nudged her puppy with her nose, helping him to squirm toward her belly so that she could feed him.

"It's awesome how animals know what to do," Mandy said. "Even first-time mothers."

"Nature is remarkable," agreed Hannah.

"Quiver's probably very thirsty now," Dr. Adam said.

"There's a bowl of fresh water in the corner," said

Michael. He was easing the soiled newspaper out of the box and replacing it with fresh sheets, being careful not to disturb Quiver and the puppy too much.

Mandy got the water and offered it to Quiver. She lapped it up and gave Mandy a grateful look before lying down again.

"That's right. You rest while you can, girl," said Hannah, glancing up from where she was busily making notes in a binder.

"What are you writing?" Mandy asked.

"I keep a record of all our pups," Hannah explained. "Everything from the time of their birth to their coloring and other individual characteristics. I also check their weight every day for the first couple of weeks."

"I wonder how many pups you're going to have to write about this time," Mandy commented. In the box, Quiver was growing restless, squirming and panting rapidly.

"The second one's on its way," said Michael.

Dr. Adam picked up the first puppy. "Let's give your mom some breathing room," he said, handing him to Hannah.

"This is my chance to weigh him," said Hannah. She put the tiny dog on a set of food scales covered in a soft cloth. "Make a note of this please, Mandy," she said as she read out the puppy's weight.

Mandy wrote down the figure next to Hannah's other notes.

"It'll probably be a few minutes before number two arrives," said Dr. Adam. "Let's have a look at this little fellow while we're waiting." He took the puppy from Hannah and felt the tiny dog's belly. Next, he looked inside his mouth and ears, listened to his breathing and heart rate, and checked his legs and paws. The puppy grunted indignantly and paddled his tiny paws; with his eyes tightly shut, he wasn't able to tell what was going on or, more important, where his mom was.

"Apart from being upset about being taken away from his food, he's as fit as a fiddle," said Dr. Adam. "Now, we need to find a babysitter until his mom's ready to have him back." He gave Mandy a questioning look.

"As if you need to ask!" Mandy smiled. She sat on the floor a little way from the box and cradled the puppy in her hands. He was so light, he felt like a baby bird.

A few moments later, the second puppy arrived, and this time Quiver took it all in stride. She cleaned the newcomer up at once and when she nudged the dark-coated pup to help it breathe, she looked up proudly at her owners as if to say, *Look, another boy. And isn't he perfect?*

"He's absolutely gorgeous," Mandy said breathlessly, admiring the puppy's almost black fur. She put the first

puppy back in the box. "Meet your brother!" she said with a smile.

The third puppy, a light gray-and-white female, arrived shortly afterward. She was as healthy as her brothers, and weighed only a few ounces less. She'd barely started feeding when Quiver began pushing out the fourth puppy.

"These pups don't waste any time," said Michael, who had only just thrown away the latest heap of soiled newspaper.

Mandy and Hannah removed the three puppies from their mother.

"Sorry, little ones," Mandy said when she was sitting with all three of them in her lap. They snuffled about as if trying to find the familiar scent of their mother. "As soon as your brother or sister is here, you can go back to your mom."

The fourth one was another healthy female with a very pale, creamy gray coat. Before long, she was snuggled up with her brothers and sister.

Mandy sat cross-legged next to the whelping box, gazing at the brand-new huskies. "You've got a beautiful family, Quiver," she said, reaching over to stroke her.

Quiver blinked and licked Mandy's hand. "She's very trusting," Mandy remarked.

"Yes, she has a wonderful temperament," agreed

Hannah. "We knew she'd make a good mother, didn't we, Michael?"

Michael smiled. "*You* knew," he said. "I'm still the rookie when it comes to huskies." He looked down at the puppies. They were bundled together, fast asleep after their energetic feeding. "I wonder if that's all of them?"

"Looks like it," said Hannah.

Mandy thought she was probably right. The last puppy had arrived half an hour ago, and Quiver looked very relaxed.

"In that case, I'll fix us all some breakfast," said Michael.

"Don't worry about feeding us," said Dr. Adam. "I'll just give Quiver a postnatal checkup, then we'll head on home."

Michael looked disappointed. "Don't rush off without breakfast. It's the least we can do to thank you."

"I don't think you should be thanking us," Mandy pointed out. "We didn't do a thing. Quiver did it all by herself."

"But you were here in case something went wrong," said Michael, "which means a lot to Hannah and me." He put his arm around Hannah's shoulders. "Now that the pups are here, we can really start concentrating on our wedding."

"When are you getting married?" Mandy asked shyly.

Hannah smiled. "On the fourteenth of February."

"Valentine's Day!" Mandy exclaimed. "What a perfect day to get married."

"Actually, we didn't only choose Valentine's Day for the romance, but also because it's the most practical," Hannah began.

"Hold on," Dr. Adam interrupted.

Mandy's heart skipped a beat. "What's wrong?"

"There's another pup on the way!" said her dad. He frowned. "It's not a good sign that it's so much later than the others, I'm afraid."

A few minutes later, the fifth puppy — pure white, and the tiniest of them all — made its entrance. Quiver looked as surprised as everyone else at the late arrival. She stared at the little bundle with her ears pricked before licking her newest baby clean.

The puppy lay very still. Too still, Mandy realized. "It's not breathing!" she cried.

Two

Biting her lip, Mandy watched her dad pick up the newborn puppy and wipe away some mucus from around its tiny muzzle. Next, he rubbed the puppy vigorously around its chest before holding it upside down and shaking it gently.

"This is a means of artificial respiration," he explained when he saw Mandy looking puzzled.

Quiver whined.

"It's all right," Mandy soothed, stroking her neck. "Dad knows what he's doing." But what she couldn't promise was that the puppy was going to be all right.

Dr. Adam put the puppy — a male — in his lap, then

12

gently pressed down on the little husky's chest. After about a minute, he stopped. There was an agonizing moment when nothing happened. But suddenly, the puppy began to breathe! His tiny rib cage was rising and falling so slightly at first that Mandy thought she might be mistaken, and was only seeing what she wanted to see. But when the puppy started to squirm, she knew she hadn't been fooling herself.

"You did it, Dad!" She felt tears of relief pricking her eyes.

Dr. Adam placed the tiny dog back in the whelping box close to Quiver's belly. The puppy must have smelled his mother's milk, because he wriggled around until he found a warm place next to her and started to feed.

Hannah flung her arms around Dr. Adam. "Thank you, thank you," she said. "See? We did need you after all."

"It was nothing," Dr. Adam said modestly. "You could have done the same thing."

Hannah leaned over the whelping box and ran a finger down the back of the pup that had given them all a scare. "Grow strong, little one." She touched each of the others next, and when she came to the second-born, the very dark-coated male, she murmured, "He's magnificent. A dead ringer for his father, Malik."

"How many dogs do you have?" Mandy asked.

"Sixteen —" began Hannah.

"Twenty-one now," Michael corrected her with a smile.

"Twenty-one!" Mandy echoed.

"It sounds like a lot," said Hannah. "But it's about right, considering that three of them are breeding females, one is retired, and twelve make up the present team. And now" — she looked fondly at the puppies — "we have five more little beauties to strengthen the team."

Team?

Michael must have seen Mandy's puzzled look. "Hannah means our dogsled team," he explained. "We compete in sled races with our huskies."

"Oh, wow!" Mandy exclaimed. "Like on Baffin Island." She was instantly transported to the snowy island off the Canadian east coast where she had raced sled dogs. She had such vivid memories of the teams of super-fit dogs pulling wooden sleds across the frozen land that she could almost hear the *swish* of the sleds' runners.

"Where do you race?" she asked Hannah.

"Sometimes in Yorkshire, when there's enough snow, but mainly in North America," answered Hannah. "We've entered the Iditarod this year."

Mandy looked at Hannah and Michael in awe. The

Iditarod was the most famous dogsled race in the world! The route led right across Alaska in early spring when thick snow still covered the land.

"That's one tough race," remarked Dr. Adam.

"One thousand and forty-nine miles from Anchorage in the east to Nome in the west," Hannah recited promptly. "Across mountains, along rivers, through gorges and canyons, in subzero temperatures for nearly two weeks."

"It sounds almost impossible," Mandy remarked.

"It's pretty tough," Hannah admitted. "Raising funds to finance the trip is half the battle, but this year I've been lucky enough to get a grant from a national sports council."

"You must spend half your life getting in shape at the gym," Dr. Adam said to Michael, "when you're not training the dogs."

"You're right about me spending a lot of time at the gym," responded Michael. "I'm the manager at Walton Fitness Center. But you're wrong about me having to get in shape. It's Hannah who's had to do it for the race. And the dogs, of course."

"Is Hannah the musher, then?" Mandy asked. She knew this was the correct term for the person who stood on the sled and controlled the dogs.

"That's right." Michael nodded. "She's the veteran around here — she's competed in the Yukon Quest four times. She's definitely more qualified than I am to do the Iditarod. Probably crazier, too!" He grinned good-naturedly at Hannah. "She can't help it, though. It's in her blood, something she was born to do. Like the dogs."

Mandy was about to ask him to explain when he turned to Hannah and said, "Should I give Quiver her breakfast now?"

"Yes, please," said Hannah.

Michael went to the kitchen, and Hannah turned to Mandy. "Want to meet the rest of the dogs?"

"I'd love to!" Mandy said enthusiastically. "Is that OK, Dad? Do we have enough time?"

"Sure," said Dr. Adam. "I still haven't given Quiver her final checkup, so you go and meet the team while I see to her."

Hannah took Mandy out onto the back porch where she switched on a floodlight. The yellow beam stretched across the yard to a large wooden building. "We converted that old cowshed into the kennel area," Hannah explained as she and Mandy walked over. "A local farmer named Steve Barker helped us."

"I know Steve," Mandy said. "He's the manager at Burnside Farm."

"He's been great at helping us settle in," said Hannah.

She pushed open the shed door and switched on a light. A chorus of excited barks and howls greeted them.

"Hi, guys!" called Hannah. "I brought a visitor."

Mandy followed her in. Two rows of spacious kennels lined the walls, and in each one a magnificent husky stood up against the wire mesh, wagging its bushy tail.

"They're gorgeous!" Mandy gasped.

"I'll introduce them to you," said Hannah, going to the first kennel. Inside was a strong-looking light gray-and-white dog with dark brown, almond-shaped eyes. "This is Galileo. Leo, for short. He's our lead dog on the team, which means he runs in front, setting the pace and showing the others the way."

Mandy reached over the wire and let Leo sniff her hand. "Hello, Galileo." When she stroked his powerful shoulders, his thick, weatherproof coat felt wonderfully soft. Leo blinked, staring at Mandy with his piercing eyes.

"You're confident, aren't you?" she commented.

"He's a born leader," said Hannah.

In the next kennel was another male, much darker than Leo. Mandy guessed this must be the puppies' father. His near-black coat was identical to that of Quiver's second-born male, and he had the deepest blue eyes Mandy had ever seen. "You must be Malik," Mandy said, stretching out her hand to him.

The dog pawed at the wire mesh and greeted Mandy with a sound that was a cross between a bark and a howl.

"Pleased to meet you, too." Mandy laughed. "He doesn't know the good news yet, does he?" she said to Hannah.

"No. And I'm not sure it'll mean a lot to him. But tell him, anyway." Hannah smiled.

"Malik, you're the lucky father of five beautiful puppies — three boys and two girls!"

Mandy could have sworn that Malik understood her. He wagged his tail faster and gave another howl-like bark.

"Congratulations!" Mandy chuckled.

There were four more males to meet: Robin, Bayonet, Odin, and Dart.

Robin was dark gray and had extraordinary eyes — one blue and the other brown. When he turned his head to one side and then to the other, it was like looking at two dogs in one! "But I'm sure you're not a mixed-up character." Mandy smiled.

"No, but he's a bit of a clown at times," Hannah said.

In the next enclosure was Bayonet, who was gray and white, with jewel-like, dark blue eyes. He was a little bigger than the others, with a powerful chest. "Hi, Bayonet," said Mandy, and when she patted him, she could feel the strength of his shoulders beneath his thick coat. "You look strong enough to pull a sled on your own."

"He practically is," said Hannah. She crouched down to look closely at Bayonet's front paws. "Hmm, his nails are a little long. I'll have to remind Michael to trim them when he has a minute. He promised to take care of the grooming while I have my hands full with the puppies."

"Don't the nails get worn down when the dogs are running?" Mandy asked.

"Not always," said Hannah, moving on to the next kennel. "They don't usually run on hard surfaces like roads. And there's a fine balance between too short and too long. The nails need to be long enough to allow for a strong grip on ice and snow, but short enough not to get caught on things."

The next dog was Odin. He was almost as dark as Malik except for his muzzle, chest, and legs, which were light gray. There were also light gray marks above his eyes that were sort of like eyebrows, Mandy thought, and his upright furry ears were outlined in black. He was certainly very handsome, but he seemed a little aloof. Instead of coming forward to meet Mandy, he sat at the back of his pen and studied her with interest.

"Sorry to barge in," Mandy apologized with a smile. There was something about Odin's attitude that made her feel like an intruder.

"Come on, Odin," said Hannah, snapping her fingers. "Don't be so unfriendly."

The handsome dog blinked and tapped his tail on the floor once or twice but stayed where he was, inspecting Mandy from a distance.

"He's very regal." Mandy laughed.

"I think his name has gone to his head," Hannah said. "Odin was the king of the Norse gods!"

They moved on to Dart, whose markings and color were similar to Odin's except for a dark, arrow-shaped stripe down his nose.

"I bet that's why you're named Dart," Mandy said, running her hand down his nose.

"That, and the fact that, given half a chance, he'll dart off after rabbits," said Hannah.

"I guess it must be pretty hard for a dog to ignore a rabbit," Mandy said.

The eight females were slightly smaller than the males, but just as striking. Alaska was the color of fresh snow with eyes like Robin's, one blue and one brown. Freya was amazingly beautiful. She was light brown with white legs and brown eyes, and seemed somewhat aloof at first, like Odin, but she thumped her tail enthusiastically when Mandy stopped to talk to her.

Dakota and Orca were both very friendly. Dakota was black with a white chest, and Orca was a very dark gray. They both had blue eyes; Dakota's were dark, and Orca's were a lighter shade.

"And this is Cindy," said Hannah. Cindy was a creamy white, and she wagged her tail so vigorously when she stood against the wire that she had to cling hard with her front paws to stop herself from falling over.

The next dog was Keira, a young one who sat down and blinked at Mandy shyly when Mandy and Hannah approached her. She was quite a bit smaller than the others and had sapphire-blue eyes and a dusky gray coat.

Mandy crouched down so that she was at the same level as Keira. She pushed her fingers through the fence. "Hi there, shy one," she whispered.

Keira gingerly stretched forward and licked Mandy's fingers so lightly it felt like a butterfly.

"You're a sweet girl," smiled Mandy, feeling her heart melt. Keira seemed so gentle, it was hard to think of her in her working role as a sled dog.

"She is sweet. And very willing," Hannah agreed.

The last two were breeding females: Indy, who was gray-blue, and her mother, Opal. As her name suggested, she was pure white.

"Opal is Robin and Keira's mother," Hannah told Mandy.

There was one more dog in the end pen, a black male with a graying muzzle, which suggested that he was older than the others. He was lying down when Mandy and Hannah approached his kennel, but he quickly stood up and stretched, greeting them with a happy wag of his tail.

"This is Havoc," said Hannah. "Our top stud dog for many years. But he's retired now."

Mandy patted the old dog. "Havoc's an unusual name," she remarked.

"It's part of a line from a play called *Julius Caesar*, by Shakespeare," Hannah told her. "'Cry havoc, and let slip the dogs of war!'" she recited.

"That's an amazing line!" Mandy said.

"Havoc is an amazing dog," said Hannah with a smile. "Robin, Freya, Bayonet, and Keira are just some of the dogs he has sired. Havoc comes from great stock, too. He's the grandson of a famous husky named War, who was the lead dog of an awesome team that won the Iditarod three times, each year in record time."

Mandy stroked Havoc's velvety ears. "It's an honor to meet a relative of such a famous dog! Where did you get Havoc?" she asked. She knew that breeders often imported top stud dogs from other countries.

"My dad gave him to us," replied Hannah, adding, "Come with me. I want to show you something in my office."

Mandy followed her through a door at the back of the kennel area. It led to a small room where leather harnesses lay in a heap on the desk next to the computer, books on the Iditarod sat stacked on chairs, jars of ointment for dogs' feet were piled on the floor, and photographs of racing teams lined the walls between shelves displaying gleaming trophies. There was no doubt that Hannah's life revolved around dogsled racing!

"Look at this," said Hannah, pointing to a photograph of a team of nine huskies. They were pulling a sled along a snow-covered track past scores of cheering spectators.

Standing on the sled was a tall, bearded man dressed in a bright yellow parka. His arms were raised high, both gloved hands rolled into fists, and there was a broad grin on his face.

"That's my father, Anthony," Hannah said proudly. "And the lead dog is War. They'd just crossed the finish line in Nome to break the previous record for the Iditarod."

So that's what Michael meant when he said that dog-sled racing was in Hannah's blood. "You're following in your father's footsteps!" Mandy remarked.

Hannah laughed. "Quite literally, too. And if I finish well, I couldn't think of a better finale to my honeymoon."

"The race doesn't sound like a very romantic honeymoon," Mandy said cautiously.

"Actually, it's not the race that's going to be our honeymoon, more the preparation time in Anchorage," Hannah explained. "That's why Valentine's Day was a good choice for the wedding. We're flying out to Alaska with the team a few days later so that we can spend two weeks getting ready for the race."

"What about the dogs left behind?" Mandy asked.

"They're going to be in very good hands," said Hannah. "My cousin Katie and her husband, Chad, are coming over from Canada for the wedding. They own huskies, too, and they'll be staying here until we get back." She looked at her watch. "The extended weather forecast will be on soon. Let's find out what kind of weather we can expect this week."

They left the kennels and hurried indoors where Michael had already switched on the TV. Dr. Adam was in the living room, too, drinking a cup of coffee.

Hannah sat on a stool in front of the TV. The weatherman said something about strong winds and heavy rain in the west, and cold dry conditions in the south, then he pointed to Yorkshire and said, "Bad news for those of you in the northeast, I'm afraid. We're expecting snow there later in the week, possibly lasting well into the weekend."

Hannah looked at Michael with shining eyes. "Not bad news for us! We can really step up our training schedule if we get lots of snow."

"I thought we'd been doing pretty well as it is," said Michael.

"Yes, but you know we need the dogs to get used to the right sled," replied Hannah, and Mandy thought she sounded a little tense. "That wooden one we're using handles completely differently than the snow runners."

"I guess so," agreed Michael. He looked at Dr. Adam.

"More coffee? Would you like some hot chocolate, Mandy?"

Dr. Adam shook his head. "No, thanks. We've got to head back now. Saturday mornings are always hectic at the clinic."

"Thanks again for everything!" said Hannah. She turned to Mandy. "How about visiting us again to see how the pups are doing?"

"I'd love that!" Mandy declared. She thought of her best friend, James Hunter, who was almost as crazy about animals as she was. "Can I bring my friend James?"

"Of course," said Hannah. "How about next Saturday? You could watch the dogs running. If the weatherman's right, we'll be training in snow."

"Can't wait!" Mandy smiled. Seven days. She was so excited about seeing these gorgeous dogs in action that she was already counting!

Three

"Is there time to visit Marble and Mandy?" Mandy asked as she and her dad passed Burnside Farm.

Marble was a dairy cow that had given birth to twins in early spring. Only one of the twins had survived. The farmer, Mr. Matthews, had named the brown-and-white calf after Mandy, who had helped feed her by hand until she was strong enough to feed from her mother.

"I guess so," said her dad. "As long as it's a *short* visit." He gave Mandy a sideways look. With mock sternness, he added, "That means no bottle feeding, no grooming, no milking . . ."

"It's a deal," Mandy promised with a grin.

Dr. Adam turned into the driveway leading to the farm. He parked in the yard outside the old stone farmhouse, and Mandy got out to knock on the door. There was no reply. "Mr. Matthews must be out," she called back to her dad. "But I'm sure he won't mind if we take a peek at the cows."

Dr. Adam nodded. "They're probably in the winter barn."

They crossed the yard to a row of outbuildings. Mandy recognized Marble and her calf as soon as they entered the first one. They were in a stall next to the door, peacefully munching hay.

Marble turned her head to look at them, chewing a piece of hay that was sticking out of her mouth. Like her calf, she was a tawny brown cow with a white blaze on her face and white patches on her sides. She mooed in greeting when she saw them. Mandy the calf had her back to them. Hearing her mother moo, she looked around. As soon as she saw the human Mandy, she came over to sniff her hand.

"You're looking great," Mandy murmured, feeling in her pocket for an edible treat. Her fingers closed on something hard and cylindrical. She took it out and was surprised to see that it was a lipstick. "Mom's coat," she realized out loud. "Sorry, no treats today," she said, patting the calf's neck.

The barn door opened and the manager, Steve, came in. "Hi, Adam. Hi, Mandy. I saw your Land Rover outside," he said. "Everything all right?"

"Everything's fine here. We've been delivering puppies at Black Tor Cottage," Mandy explained. Mandy the calf must have felt left out because she began to nibble Mandy's fingers. Mandy giggled and pulled her hand away. "I think you'll find the hay a lot tastier."

"Were you delivering Quiver's puppies?" Steve guessed.

"Yes. Five little beauties," Dr. Adam told him.

Steve smiled. "I can't wait to see them. Hannah's going to have her hands really full now, with the wedding coming up and everything."

Mandy noticed that he was wearing a tool belt with a hammer, a bundle of nails, and a pair of wire cutters. "Are you doing more work on the huskies' kennels this morning?"

"Not right now," Steve said, frowning. "I'm building a new cage for my ferrets."

"You have ferrets?" Mandy said excitedly. Some people thought they were mean, smelly creatures, but she didn't agree with that at all. Ferrets were wonderful pets: lively, affectionate, and very sweet.

"I do, indeed. Come and see them." Steve started toward the door.

Mandy gave Marble and her calf a last pat each, then hurried after Steve. But a cough from her dad stopped her. "Ahem!" He tapped his watch. "What about our deal?"

"It's just for a minute," Mandy pleaded.

"Or five," Dr. Adam said, sighing, but he followed Mandy to Steve's cottage on the other side of the yard.

The ferrets were in the living room with Steve's wife, Lisa. A lovely peach-colored ferret was in her lap, and the other was in a cage on the floor.

"Look, visitors for you, Fizz and Charm." Lisa smiled.

The ferrets stared at the strangers suspiciously.

"Which is which?" Mandy asked, going over to sit on the sofa next to Lisa.

"This one is Fizz," replied Lisa, stroking the ferret in her lap. "He's the hob, or male. And that's Charm, the jill, or female, in the cage."

Charm was dark brown and, like Fizz, very beautiful. Their fur was soft and thick, and their long bodies were the perfect shape for what they would do in the wild — enter rabbit burrows.

Mandy felt a little uncomfortable thinking about this. She knew that most people kept ferrets as pets, but sometimes country folk used them to hunt rabbits and rats. She hoped this wasn't the case with Fizz and Charm. "You don't, um, use them —" she began.

"For hunting?" Lisa finished the sentence for her.

Mandy nodded as she reached out to Fizz and began to stroke him. The little creature scrambled onto Mandy's lap, enjoying the attention.

"Hunting! Not on your life," said Steve. "They're only pets."

"I suppose they're easier than dogs because you don't have to walk them or train them," remarked Dr. Adam, scratching Charm's head through the wire.

"I guess so. But they can be quite a handful at times!" said Lisa. She dipped a cotton swab into a small bottle of olive oil. "Do you mind if I take Fizz back for a minute, Mandy?" she asked. "I need to clean his ears."

"Sure." Mandy handed the hob to his owner. "Do their ears get very dirty?"

"No more than any other animal's," said Lisa, carefully wiping the cotton swab inside Fizz's ears. "But it's a great way to use their natural behavior to keep them in check, and make them understand who's boss around here. You see, dominant ferrets do all the ear cleaning in a family."

Mandy was intrigued. "That means they see you as the top dog — I mean, ferret."

"That's right," said Lisa with a grin.

"Oh, great! A wife who thinks she's a ferret," joked Steve. "But seriously," he added, "now that we have a

third one, we really need to make sure they're well controlled."

"A third one? Where?" Mandy looked around.

"I'll go get him," said Steve. He went out and came back with a small blue-gray ferret wriggling in his hands. "Meet Teal, the baby of the family. He arrived only yesterday so he's not as tame as the others yet."

To Mandy's delight, Steve put the young ferret in her lap. Teal sat very still with his shoulders hunched. "Don't worry, little one," Mandy whispered, stroking him. "I won't hurt you." Teal looked up at her, his bright, dark eyes studying her closely. "He has the cutest face," Mandy said.

Dr. Adam tapped his watch again. "Remember our deal, Mandy? Time to go." He came over to pick up Teal from Mandy's lap. Suddenly, the room filled with an unpleasant musky odor.

"Oh, dear!" said Lisa. "I think you must have scared him. It seems like he emptied his scent glands."

"I'm very insulted," Dr. Adam chuckled. "But you'll probably want to do something about that antisocial behavior. We can remove the scent glands very easily if you like."

"That's right," said Steve. "Fizz and Charm had theirs removed before they came to live with us."

"Then bring Teal down to the clinic soon and we'll do it," offered Dr. Adam. "We'll also vaccinate him against distemper."

"I thought only dogs could get distemper," Mandy said.

"Dogs are most at risk," her dad agreed, "but other animals can catch it, too. It can be especially serious in ferrets, so we need to make sure this little one is protected."

"Will do," said Steve, taking Teal from Mandy.

"I'll call the clinic and make an appointment for next week."

"See you then," Mandy said as she and her dad went outside.

Dr. Adam had just started up the engine when Mr. Matthews pulled up in his Land Rover. "Good morning," he said, frowning. "Is anything wrong?" He sneezed as he spoke and took out a handkerchief to blow his nose.

"Not at all," said Dr. Adam cheerfully. "We've just been saying hello to some old friends."

"And three new ones," Mandy put in.

"Steve's ferrets?"

Mandy nodded. "They're absolutely adorable."

"Yes, especially the youngster," agreed Mr. Matthews. "But I don't think he's warmed up to me yet. He gave me a good dose of his warning scent when I got too close!" He chuckled as he got out of the Land Rover, but another bout of sneezing interrupted him. "Oh, this cold," he muttered, and blew his nose again before opening the back of the Land Rover to take out a heavy roll of fencing wire.

"Here. Let me do that for you," offered Dr. Adam, cutting the engine and getting out. "You're looking a little under the weather."

"I feel it, too," said the farmer, wiping his streaming eyes. "I've been trying to shake this cold off for a week, but it's gotten worse."

"Maybe you should go to bed," Mandy suggested.

Mr. Matthews shrugged. "Easier said than done. Farmers can't just take to their beds when they feel sick."

"But Steve's here," Mandy argued.

Mr. Matthews coughed. "Just as well," he wheezed. "I'm going to need the pair of extra hands now that snow is in the forecast for the weekend." He shook his head and muttered through gritted teeth, "That's all I need right now. Six feet of snow."

Mandy didn't share his gloomy sentiments. More than anything else, she wanted it to snow over the weekend, so she could experience the thrill of authentic dogsled racing once again!

Mandy didn't have to wait until the weekend before she saw the huskies. When she and James arrived home from school on Thursday afternoon, Dr. Adam was getting into the Land Rover with his vet's bag.

"Where are you going?" Mandy asked.

"Black Tor Cottage. Hannah called to say that Quiver's not well."

Less than a minute later, Mandy and James were in the Land Rover, their schoolbags abandoned in the garage.

"No one wants to come with me?" Dr. Adam teased.

"If we must," joked James.

As they drove past Burnside Farm, Mandy suggested they stop by after they'd seen Quiver to remind Steve about Teal's distemper injection. She was sure he wouldn't have forgotten, but it was also a way for James to meet the ferrets!

"No need," said Dr. Adam, spoiling Mandy's plan. "Steve called this morning and made an appointment for Monday."

Hannah was waiting for them at the door of the cottage. She must have heard the Land Rover winding up the steep road. Mandy thought she looked as if she hadn't slept for days. Her face was drawn and pale, and there were dark rings under her eyes.

"I'm desperately worried about Quiver," Hannah said. "She's not eating her food, and I think she's just had a fit."

Mandy's heart sank. "What about the puppies?"

"I think they're OK," said Hannah. "But they're crying a lot."

"Let's have a look at them," said Dr. Adam, hurrying through to the puppy room.

Michael was sitting on the floor next to the whelping box, stroking Quiver's head. The five puppies squirmed at their mother's side, nosing around as if they were hungry. It was such a different picture from the last time Mandy had seen them.

"We'll need to take the puppies away so I can examine her thoroughly," said Dr. Adam, opening his bag.

"I'll take them into the living room," Michael offered, and he picked up three of them. "Would you mind bringing the others?" he asked Mandy and James.

Mandy bent down and carefully scooped up the tiny white male. In just four days, he had grown a lot and his coat had fluffed out so that he felt sturdy and soft in Mandy's hands.

James picked up the black male, the one Hannah said was a dead ringer for his father, Malik. "They're so tiny, it's hard to think of them pulling a sled someday," he remarked.

They put the puppies on a blanket in front of the fire. Like Hannah's office, the living room was crowded with all sorts of dog gear as well as wedding gifts that hadn't been unwrapped yet. Mandy sat on the floor with her back to the fire, to make sure the puppies didn't crawl too close.

"You must be James," said Michael, shaking his hand.

"Nice to meet you," James said politely. "And it's good to meet them, too." He nodded at the puppies tumbling about on the rug.

Mandy bit her lip. Quiver had looked terrible. The mention of a fit was extremely worrying, too. She'd been in great condition four days ago. How could she have gotten sick so quickly? "I hope Dad can find out what's wrong with Quiver," she said, sighing.

"You know he will," James said confidently. "Your dad's an awesome vet."

"Yes, he is," Mandy agreed. *But sometimes even awesome vets can't help a sick animal*, she added silently.

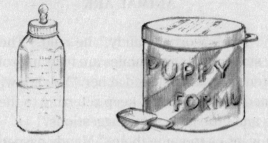

Four

Lost in her thoughts, Mandy didn't notice the white puppy crawling toward her until she felt him bump against her leg. When she picked him up, he grunted softly and started to suck on her finger.

"Poor little guy," Mandy said. "You're really hungry, aren't you?"

Three of the other puppies had curled up together and were fast asleep, while the fifth one, the light gray-and-white female, was snuggled up in the crook of James's knee.

Michael ran his finger gently over the dark male puppy, who was sleeping on his back with his paws in the air. "Don't worry, Mandy," he said. "They're not exactly starving. Their tummies are nice and round." He straightened up and beamed at her. "You know, it's time we named them. We can't keep referring to them as little girls and little guys. Any suggestions?"

"You want us to name them?" Mandy gasped, feeling very honored.

"Of course. After all, you were one of the midwives, and James looks like he'll become a vet, too!" Michael smiled at James who had picked up the gray-and-white puppy and was holding her against his cheek. "Any ideas?"

"I guess we should think about snow and ice and sleds and running and things like that," said James.

"Not necessarily," Michael told him. "Hannah and I have also used names from Norse mythology."

"Like Odin," Mandy said, remembering.

"Yes, and Freya's another one. According to Norse myths, she's the goddess of love and beauty," said Michael.

Mandy pictured the beautiful brown husky. "She really lives up to that name."

With his free hand, James took off his glasses and cleaned them on his sweater. "But I don't know anything about Norse mythology."

"We use other sources, too," said Michael. "Like

atlases, fairy tales . . . but sometimes we choose a name that suits the puppy's appearance or personality. Or we might just like a name and hope the puppy grows into it."

"Like Keira," Mandy suggested. Somehow the name seemed to match the shy dog's sweet nature.

They sat in silence for a few minutes, trying to think of ideas.

James held the gray-and-white puppy away from his cheek and looked at it. "What about Alaska for this one?"

"There's one named that already," Mandy said.

"OK, then. Aspen?" James tried again. "That's a ski resort in Colorado, isn't it?"

Michael nodded. "Yes, good choice."

Mandy studied the three puppies on the mat. The color of the very dark male reminded her of a very deep lake. Caspian, an inland sea she'd studied in a geography class, came to mind. "Caspian?" she suggested to Michael.

"Perfect!" he agreed.

There were still three names to choose. Michael came up with Vali for the firstborn pup, the light-colored male. "The name of another Norse god," he explained.

The pale, creamy gray female was curled up next to Vali. She stretched, yawned, then went back to sleep.

"Her color makes me think of a ghost," said James. "How about Spirit?"

"I like it," said Michael. "But some friends of ours named one of their dogs that."

"Phantom?" James persisted.

Mandy and Michael exchanged a look of approval. "Not bad. Not bad at all," said Michael.

There was only one pup still unnamed — the one in Mandy's arms. Although she adored the others, she had to admit that the tiny puppy — the one who might not have made it — was quickly becoming her favorite. As she gazed at him, a name came to her. "Nemo," she said quietly.

James frowned. "Doesn't that mean *no one* in Latin?"

"I think so," Mandy replied. "But when you think about it, he almost *was* no one."

"Then Nemo it is!" said Michael.

They were running through the five names again when the door opened and Dr. Adam came in.

"Is Quiver OK?" Mandy blurted out.

"She will be soon," he answered.

Mandy felt as if the whole world sighed with relief.

"It's hypocalcemia," her dad went on and, seeing the puzzled looks on all their faces, he added, "Milk fever, caused when a nursing mother's blood calcium drops."

"Can you treat her?" asked Michael.

"I already have, with a calcium injection. She'll be as good as new in a couple of hours," said Dr. Adam. "We'll just need to keep an eye on her."

Nemo started to squirm in Mandy's hands. "When can the puppies go back to Quiver?" Mandy asked. She offered Nemo her little finger again, but this time he turned his head away as if he knew there wasn't any food there.

"After they've eaten," her dad replied. "We're going to have to bottle-feed them for a few days because Quiver's milk supply has been affected. Hannah's in the kitchen right now preparing the formula I brought."

If Mandy hadn't been holding Nemo, she would have flung her arms around her dad. "James said you were an awesome vet, and he's right! What about bottles, though?"

"I brought those, too," said Dr. Adam. "And I may be wrong," he added with a wink, "but I'm pretty sure I also brought along a couple of volunteers who'd be prepared to help feed the pups."

"Right again," Mandy said, grinning. She stroked Nemo's head. "Not long now," she told him. "Then your tummy will be full again."

Hannah appeared then with five small bottles of formula. She handed one to each person. "Luckily, there are five of us," she said as she watched Dr. Adam pick up Caspian and move a stack of books off a chair so that he could sit down. "That means all the pups can be fed at the same time. They'll have to stand in line if I'm the only one here."

Mandy put the bottle in front of Nemo's nose. "Try this. It's a lot more tasty than my finger."

Nemo moved his head away, uninterested. Mandy squirted some formula onto her hand and dipped the bottle into it. "Come on, Nemo. Try it." This time, the puppy sniffed the bottle, but he still seemed rather uncertain. "It's milk, Nemo," said Mandy, and she gently rubbed the nipple against his mouth, at the same time squirting out a few more drops of formula.

Suddenly, Nemo got the idea and latched onto the bottle.

"There." Mandy smiled. "I told you it was better than my finger."

When the puppies had been fed, Mandy and James carried them back to their mother. Quiver was lying in the whelping box but as soon as she saw everyone coming in, she lifted her head.

"You look a lot better already," Mandy told her. Quiver wasn't trembling like she'd been earlier, and she seemed a lot more alert. "I bet you're wondering where your

babies are." Mandy let Quiver sniff Nemo and Caspian before she put them in the box next to her.

Quiver sniffed each one, then nosed them each again as if she was counting them.

"All present," promised James, smoothing Quiver's head. "I think we did a good job of being stand-in mothers."

"They're going to need stand-in moms for a few more days yet, aren't they?" Hannah asked Dr. Adam. She sounded very tired. Apart from a litter of puppies to hand-feed, there were the other dogs to care for, in addition to training for the Iditarod, as well as her wedding to plan in just over a week's time.

"They'll need to feed several times a day until Quiver's back to normal," Dr. Adam confirmed. He glanced at the clock on the wall. It was five-fifteen. "We should be on our way now," he said to Mandy and James.

Mandy pet Quiver one last time, then stood up to go. Michael seemed to be getting ready to go out, too. He picked up his jacket that had been draped over a corner of the whelping box, as if he'd flung it there in a hurry.

"I'd better head back to work," he said. "You'll be able to handle this until I get off tonight?" he asked Hannah.

Hannah sighed. "I'll have to."

"I'm sorry," said Michael. He put his arm around her

shoulders. "I know you're under a lot of pressure, and you know I'd help out more if I could. But with the honeymoon coming up, I can't take any extra time off."

"I know." Hannah shrugged his arm away and checked the heater to make sure it was the right temperature for the puppies. "It's just that I'm not sure how I'll fit everything in."

Mandy didn't even hesitate. A gorgeous family of huskies and their owners were in trouble. "We'll help you," she offered at once. "Won't we, James?"

"Definitely!"

"We'll come after school to feed the puppies and clean out the whelping box," Mandy continued.

"And take Quiver out for short walks," added James.

"And help with the other dogs," Mandy added.

"We could even help with their training," James suggested hopefully.

Dr. Adam grinned. "I think taking a team of huskies on a training run is being a little ambitious," he commented. "Even for a pair of animal experts like you two."

James blushed. "I'm sure there's *something* we could do to help the team," he said. "Like, like . . ."

"Like cheering them on?" Michael said. "I know Hannah and the team would love that, wouldn't you?"

Hannah smiled, making some of the tension in her face drain away. "We certainly would. And I would be really grateful if you could come after school to help with the puppies."

"We'll be here as soon as we can tomorrow after-noon," Mandy promised.

"Oh, one other thing," said Hannah. "Keep your fingers crossed for snow!"

Mandy held up both hands with her fingers firmly crossed. "It'll be hard to do any work at school like this," she said, chuckling, "but they're staying crossed until the first flakes start falling."

She didn't have to keep her fingers crossed for long. As she stepped outside, a delicate white shape fluttered down in front of her. "A snowflake!" she cried, and then another wafted down onto her hand. *Keep it up!* she begged silently. She couldn't wait to see Hannah's team pulling a sled across a snow-covered field!

Five

"That'll do, Nemo," Mandy said, laughing. She was sitting on the floor in the puppy room feeding Nemo. He had drained every drop of formula and was still sucking the bottle as hard as he could. "Just because you're the smallest doesn't mean you need any more than the others!"

It was the next afternoon, and Mandy and James were back at Black Tor Cottage. To their disappointment, the hint of snow the day before had turned out to be a false alarm. The new day had dawned cold, dry, and gloomy, but not decked in white as Mandy had hoped.

But at least the dry weather meant they could bicycle to school rather than take the bus. That way, they were able to go straight to the cottage on their way home.

Mandy gently took the bottle away from Nemo, then put him back in the box with Vali, Phantom, and Aspen, who had already been fed. James was still feeding Caspian, who was holding the neck of the nearly empty bottle with his tiny front paws.

"To think these tiny paws will be running across ice and snow one day," he marveled.

"It's amazing," Mandy agreed. "Especially when the puppies' eyes aren't even open yet."

"They'll open after about ten days, right?" asked James.

"About that," Mandy agreed. "So the puppies have four more days before they find out what we look like!"

Mandy was collecting the empty bottles when Hannah came in. She'd taken Quiver out for a walk while the puppies were feeding.

"Quiver looks even better today," Mandy commented. The young dog's recovery had been dramatic, thanks to the calcium injection, even though the puppies would need to be bottle-fed until their mom had all her strength back.

Quiver must have realized that one of her pups was missing. She looked around anxiously until she saw

Caspian in James's lap. She stared at James with a pleading expression.

"OK, you can have your son back now," James said, putting Caspian into the box.

Caspian wriggled around until he was curled up against Nemo. But this disturbed Nemo. He grunted, too, then rolled onto his back and fell asleep again with his woolly little legs sticking straight up in the air.

"I wish I'd brought my camera with me." James sighed.

"There's always tomorrow," said Hannah. "You'll able to take some shots of the team in action, too."

"But probably not on snow," Mandy said gloomily. "I must have uncrossed my fingers too soon."

"No, you didn't," said Hannah. "Look." She pointed to the window.

Mandy and James looked outside. "It's snowing!" they exclaimed.

Their bikes were leaning against the wall on the far side of the yard. The seats and handlebars had turned white, and the bottoms of the wheels looked as if they'd been cut off where the snow was piled up around them.

"It's coming down hard," said Mandy. "We'd better head home soon." She started toward the kitchen, intending to sterilize the bottles before she left.

Hannah stopped her. "Don't worry, Mandy. I'll do that. You and James had better go."

"Are you sure?" asked James. "I mean, isn't there anything else you'd like us to do? Like feed the other dogs?" Mandy realized that he still hadn't met them.

"I'll be fine," Hannah replied wearily. "Mike should be here in an hour. And you've done the most important job." She looked down at the sleeping heap of huskies.

"Then we'll see you tomorrow," said Mandy, picking up her jacket that was on a large cardboard box labeled BOOTIES.

James frowned. "Have you knitted booties for the puppies like people do for human babies?"

Hannah burst out laughing. "Booties for the puppies! Oh, that's funny." She opened the box and took out what looked like a small pair of black rubber socks. "They're for the sled team, to protect their feet during the race. We go through hundreds of pairs, so it's one of our biggest expenses."

James blushed, and Hannah put an arm around him so that he blushed even more.

"There was no way for you to know that," she said kindly. "There's so much to dog racing that even I don't know all of it yet. And thanks for the laugh. I really needed that."

"That's OK," muttered James, still blushing. Pulling

on his jacket, he said, "Come on, Mandy. We'd better go before we get snowed in."

On Saturday morning, Mandy woke up to a real winter wonderland.

"I know it makes things hard for farmers like Mr. Matthews," she said when her mom was driving her and James up to the cottage. "But I can't help being glad about the snow if it means we get to see the huskies in action!"

Dr. Emily downshifted to a lower gear. "I'm sure Mr. Matthews is fine. He has Steve to help him."

"I hope they don't get snowed in," Mandy said. "Teal's having his vaccination on Monday."

"The roads might be plowed by then," said Dr. Emily. She carefully eased the Land Rover through a drift that swept over the hedge like a breaking wave.

James peered out of the window. "We should have put chains on the wheels."

"We'll be all right," Dr. Emily said grimly as the Land Rover surged forward again.

A few minutes later, they pulled up outside the house. It had been transformed from an ordinary stone building to something that looked as if it belonged on a Christmas card. The snow in the yard was pristine except for two sets of footprints — one from a dog and the other from a person.

Quiver and Michael, Mandy guessed, noticing that the human prints were a little too big to be Hannah's.

"I'll just check Quiver, then be on my way," said Dr. Emily, taking her vet's bag out of the back of the car.

"She looks all right to me," Mandy said.

James frowned. "How do you know? You can't see her."

"No, but she's been out for a walk this morning," Mandy said, pointing to the tracks in the snow.

James grinned. "Good work, Detective Mandy."

"Really tough," Mandy joked. She was about to knock on the door when she heard angry voices coming from inside.

"I can't believe you did that, Michael," Hannah was saying. "How hard can it be to read a few simple instructions?"

"I told you, I couldn't find them. This place is such a mess that it's a miracle if I find anything, let alone a piece of paper," Michael retorted.

"Well, you should have checked with me. I can't do everything, you know. It'll be your home, too, soon," Hannah snapped. "There's nothing stopping you from cleaning up."

"I don't have time. I've been up since five this morning and I've got to be at work in twenty minutes."

"And that's more important than the dogs and their health, right?" Hannah shot back angrily.

"No, but my job *is* important," said Michael.

Mandy felt very uncomfortable. She wondered if she should knock on the door to let Michael and Hannah know they'd arrived. But Dr. Emily had heard the argument, too. She beckoned to Mandy and James and they went back to the Land Rover.

"We'll wait here," said Dr. Emily. "We don't want to eavesdrop."

Soon after that, the door opened and Michael came out, yanking on his jacket. He saw Mandy and her mom and James standing by the Land Rover and gave them a fleeting wave. Mandy waved back, but Michael was

already swinging open the garage doors. Inside was a black van with stickers on the back window announcing that racing huskies were in transit. Michael climbed in, slammed the driver's door, and turned on the engine. He backed out and drove away, skidding as he steered out of the driveway.

"Wedding jitters probably," said Dr. Emily as she went toward the front door again. "But it's none of our business."

As it turned out, it *was* their business. Hannah appeared in the doorway, looking more worried than angry. "I'm so glad you're here, Emily," she said. "I need you to check some of the dogs for me."

"Sure," said Dr. Emily. "I suppose you mean Quiver."

"Well, yes," said Hannah. She glanced toward the road where the van could be heard winding its way down the steep hill. "But right now I'm more concerned about Orca, Alaska, and Robin."

Mandy's heart lurched.

"They've had the wrong rations," Hannah went on, leading the way to the kitchen. "I only noticed after Michael had fed them."

Mandy swapped a relieved glance with James. Incorrect rations could hardly be a disaster.

Hannah guessed what they were thinking and corrected them. "It could be disastrous," she warned.

"We're weaning the dogs on to their racing diet, which is high in fat and protein." She picked up a plastic packet from the tabletop. "Michael gave them each a whole pack of concentrated food, instead of just a portion."

Mandy heard her mom quietly suck in her breath. "Not good news," she murmured. "Too much concentrated food can lead to kidney damage."

Tears welled in Hannah's eyes. "I know. But Michael doesn't — didn't. Until now." She shook her head. "I should have fed them myself."

"Let's see how serious it is," Dr. Emily said calmly.

"I'd really appreciate it if you could sit with Quiver and the pups," Hannah said to Mandy and James. "Quiver's a little nervous after . . ." She sighed. "After Mike and I, er, argued."

"Sure," said Mandy, even though she was desperate to know how the three racing dogs were.

Quiver was lying with her puppies in the whelping box, watching the door as if she were waiting for Michael and Hannah to return. When she saw Mandy and James come in, she thumped her tail against the side of the box. The puppies were snuggled up next to her, twitching in their sleep.

"I wonder why they twitch like that," said James. "It's like they're dreaming."

"Maybe," said Mandy, smoothing Quiver's thick coat. "But Mom said that it also means they're doing well."

They sat on the floor and spoke soothingly to Quiver, stroking her until she stopped watching the door and drifted off to sleep. But as soon as Quiver heard Hannah's voice, she opened her eyes and sat up.

"Thanks so much, Emily," Hannah was saying. "I can't tell you how relieved I am."

"They seem fine. It was just one time, so their systems should cope. Still, I'd keep them quiet for a day or two," advised Dr. Emily. "Quiver's turn now!" she announced as she came into the puppy room. She checked the new mother over before declaring that she was well on the road to recovery.

Hannah looked as if a load had been lifted from her shoulders, especially when Dr. Emily said that the puppies should be able to start feeding from their mother in a day or two.

"Things are beginning to look up," said Hannah. "Let's go out for a training run to celebrate!"

"We'll get the sled out first," Hannah decided as they crunched across the snow toward the kennels.

Dr. Emily had left and was coming back later to get Mandy and James.

Hannah had changed into a red parka, with a black

wool hat pulled over her ears, red ski pants, and boots. She stopped at a shed just beyond the kennels and opened the door. There were two sleds inside: a wooden one on wheels, and a streamlined-looking one on runners.

"Here it is," Hannah announced, running her hand along the handle of the streamlined vehicle. "The sled that'll be first across the finish line in Nome next month!"

"It looks a little like a hammock on skis," James observed, going over to help Hannah drag the sled into the yard.

Mandy thought James's description was perfect. The aluminum frame supported what looked like a cross between a deck chair and a hammock made from strong black fabric.

"The hammock part is called the cargo bed," Hannah explained. "It carries all the food, booties, clothes, medication — everything we'll need between checkpoints."

They pulled the sled to the kennels. It ran as smoothly as silk on its aluminum runners. "For the race, I'll put plastic on the bottom of the runners to make them slide even better over the snow," said Hannah.

The sled had a plastic bumper that Hannah called a brushbow. "It takes the brunt of any collisions we might have with trees, bushes, or other sleds," she said. She must have noticed Mandy and James trading a look of alarm because she added, "Most of the time I can stop the dogs in time to prevent a crash. There's a brake as well as a snow hook, which is a little like an anchor. And see that rubber mat between the runners? That's called a drag, which also helps slow the team down."

"It's pretty high-tech," said James admiringly.

"Not your average plastic toboggan," Mandy joked.

"Plastic toboggans are a good start, though," said Hannah. She signaled to James to stop pulling and picked up a thick rope that was attached to the back of the sled. She looped it around a strong metal post set into the ground.

"Is that to stop the dogs from charging off too soon?" James guessed.

"That's right. It's called the snub line," said Hannah. "It has a quick-release mechanism so we can make an instant start." She showed Mandy and James how it worked. "Would you like to be in charge of it today, James?"

"You bet!" He grinned.

"OK. Let's get the gang line untangled," said Hannah. She took a heap of ropes out of the cargo bed and stretched it out on the ground in front of the sled. Mandy saw that the pile of ropes was actually a long, thick line with other lines connected to either side of it, and one at the front.

"These side lines, the tug lines, connect the dogs' harnesses to the main line," Hannah explained. She pointed out the neck lines that attached each dog's collar to the gang line. "They stop the dogs from going too far out to the side."

James picked up a giant rubber band that was fixed to the back of the towline. "This looks like a bungee cord," he said.

"It's the shock cord," said Hannah. "It stretches between the sled and the rest of the gang line to absorb the impact if there is a collision. That way the dogs don't get jarred."

This was exactly the sort of information Mandy liked to hear about! The more features there were to protect the dogs from harm, the better, as far as she was concerned.

"Let's get the dogs now," said Hannah. She opened the door and a chorus of excited howls met them.

"Who's coming for a run?" called Hannah as the chorus grew louder and more frenzied.

Mandy resisted the urge to throw back her head and howl like a husky, too. She was as excited as they were at the thought of a race through the snow!

Six

"Mandy, would you get Keira, please?" asked Hannah. "And James, you bring Odin."

"Sure," Mandy answered, delighted at the chance to get to know the shy husky better.

Keira seemed glad to see Mandy, too. She jumped up against the wire of her enclosure and whined excitedly.

"Hi there, girl," Mandy said, opening the gate. "Ready to go?"

She was a bit wary that Keira might make a bolt past her to get to the snow, but the husky trotted quietly out of the kennel block and stood stock-still next to Mandy while she clipped the tug line and neck line into place.

"You're an angel," Mandy said, patting her when she'd finished.

Keira licked Mandy's face and wagged her tail.

The dogs around her were much more excited, clamoring and pulling at their harnesses, eager to start. Mandy had brought out Malik earlier, while Hannah and James hitched Dart and Dakota to the line. Hannah had gone back in to get Cindy and was just coming out of the kennels with her now.

James was having a hard time controlling Odin. Instead of being aloof and hard to read like yesterday, he was howling like a wolf and jerking on his lead until he almost pulled James off his feet.

"Jeez, he's strong!" James puffed, finally managing to clip Odin's collar to the tug line.

Odin lunged forward, his paws scrabbling in the snow, making it impossible for James to attach the neck line.

"A treat might make him stand still," Mandy suggested.

"I'll give it a try," said James, fishing in his pocket for one of the dog biscuits he always carried with him.

But Odin continued to leap around, knocking James's hand and sending the biscuit flying. Odin clearly had only one thing on his mind — running!

Hannah connected Cindy to the towline. "Let me give you a hand," she said to James. She expertly used her knees to keep the dog still while James snapped the neck line onto his collar.

With Odin in place, there was only one more dog to be attached: Leo, the leader. When he walked out next to Hannah, Mandy was sure he knew just how important he was! He strutted to the front of the line, his shoulder muscles flexing under his thick gray fur.

James took a photo of the harnessed team. Cindy and Dart were at the back; Hannah called them the wheel dogs because they helped to steer the sled. The next pair were Dakota and Odin — team dogs whose job was to follow the dogs in front of them, steadily pulling as they ran. In front of them were Keira and Malik — the swing dogs who not only helped the leader set the pace but also assisted in turning the team.

And at the head was Leo, the only dog not running in tandem with another. He had to listen to the musher's commands, find the trail, and set the pace, while keeping the team on that same trail. No wonder he knew he was important!

There were several empty places along the main line that could have been filled by five other dogs to make up a team of twelve. But Hannah was running only seven dogs today. This was partly because the three who'd been incorrectly fed were being rested, and also because, as Hannah explained, taking the full team was risky.

"They're so fit and strong and raring to go," she said, "that even eight dogs could pull me from here to Scotland in no time at all! Of course, I'll have to cope with all of them in the race, but for now I prefer to keep on the safe side."

Seeing the dogs straining impatiently in their places, Mandy was sure Hannah wasn't exaggerating. It was a miracle they hadn't managed to snap the snub line already.

Hannah had a pair of goggles slung around her neck. She put them on and pulled up the hood of her parka. "James, stand by at the snub line," she said. "And Mandy, open the gate, please."

Mandy ran to the big wooden gate and swung it open. When the dogs saw the snowy field stretching ahead of them, their yelping reached a deafening pitch. *Let's go!* they must have been screaming.

"All right, all right," Hannah shouted, and she went around to the back of the sled and stood on the footboards that were fixed to the runners. "OK, James!" she called.

James flicked the quick-release mechanism and the snub line snapped away from the post.

"Hike up!" Hannah cried, and the dogs burst forward, jerking the sled as if it were a feather.

They hurtled through the gate so fast that Mandy

caught only a glimpse of Hannah's face, but that was enough to see she looked happier than ever. As the dogs charged forward, Mandy recalled the line from the Shakespeare play. "'Cry havoc, and let slip the dogs of war!'" she shouted at the top of her voice.

James stared at her like she was crazy.

"I'll explain later," Mandy told him.

"Gee!" called Hannah, leaning to one side. The team obeyed at once, swerving to the right to avoid a big flat rock.

"Straight ahead!" Hannah shouted, and Leo led his team forward as straight as an arrow.

"Let's go after them!" yelled James, running through the gate.

Mandy didn't think they stood much chance of catching up but she raced off, following the paw prints that twenty-eight husky feet had left in the snow.

They jogged along the track for about ten minutes, the distance between them and the team growing bigger all the time. Just when it looked like Hannah was taking them into the field beyond, Mandy saw that the dogs turned sharply to the left and kept turning until they faced the way they'd come. "They're coming back!" she said.

A moment later the dogs were just a few feet away, their breath steaming around their muzzles like puffy white clouds.

"Whoa!" Hannah called, but the dogs weren't ready to stop yet and thundered on so that Mandy and James had to leap off the track and into the soft heaps of snow at the side to get out of their way.

"Whoa!" Hannah shouted again, and she must have jammed on the brake, or stepped onto the drag — or even both — because the team came to a stop just past Mandy and James.

"They're like thunder!" said Hannah, pushing her goggles up onto her head. Her face was flushed and her eyes sparkled with excitement.

James looked puzzled. "Is that all the training you're doing for the day?"

"Oh, no," said Hannah. "I thought we'd put some weight in the cargo bed, to give the dogs a sense of the load they'll be pulling in Alaska."

"Do you want us to get some stuff?" Mandy offered.

"No, I've got all I need here." Hannah smiled.

"Us?" James gasped.

"Yep! Who's first?"

Mandy knew that James was dying to go. "James," she said at the same time that he said, "Mandy."

"No, you go first," Mandy said. After all, she had been on a dogsled before, on Baffin Island, so she could wait a little longer to go again.

But James insisted she have the first turn. "I'll wait for the dogs to get rid of some of that energy," he joked.

Mandy didn't want to waste any more time arguing. She climbed into the cargo bed and sat down.

"Are you sure they'll be able to pull the extra weight?" James asked doubtfully. Mandy pulled a face at him. She wasn't *that* heavy!

"Oh, yeah," said Hannah. "They're in such good shape, they could pull a small car right now."

A small car! "No way!" was all Mandy had time to say because Hannah yelled, "Hike up!" and Mandy felt a sudden jerk as the sled shot forward.

"Haw!" Hannah commanded, and the dogs veered to the left and kept turning until they rejoined the track across the field.

"Straight on!" called Hannah, and Leo thundered forward.

As they flew past James, Mandy saw him raise his camera and say something, but his voice was drowned by the swish of the runners and the rhythmic panting of the dogs. Her view ahead was filled with a blur of legs and fur and strong shoulders and backs. It had to be one of the most amazing sights she had ever seen!

The team raced down a gentle slope, passing a pair of very surprised crows that took off in a flurry.

"Sorry to bother you!" Mandy yelled, laughing.

The team turned left and followed a stream that cut across the field. The cold air slammed into Mandy's face, freezing her cheeks and lips. She closed her eyes for a moment. With the icy wind stinging her eyelids, and her ears filled with the sound of the sled and the galloping huskies, it was easy to imagine she wasn't in Yorkshire, but far away in Alaska, competing in the Iditarod!

"That was incredible!" said James.

Mandy grinned at him. It was at least the fifth time he'd said it since they'd returned to Hannah's house.

They'd helped her to unhitch the dogs before rubbing them down. Under Hannah's watchful eye, they'd fed the team and given them fresh water. Now the three of them were in the kitchen, drinking hot chocolate.

"Maybe you could train Blackie to be a sled dog," Mandy teased. Blackie was James's Labrador.

"Oh, yeah. Then I *would* get pulled to Scotland!" James laughed and Mandy joined him.

The phone rang and Hannah picked it up. "Oh, hey, honey," she said. Mandy guessed it was Michael on the other end.

She tried not to listen, but she couldn't help hearing words like "sorry," "anxious," and "stress," then phrases like "great run" and "successful session." When Hannah hung up and sat down smiling, Mandy knew that she and Michael had put their argument behind them.

"Great news!" Hannah announced. "Michael's managed to change his shifts so he can be here to help me in the mornings and early evenings. And he's going to try to be here for more training sessions, too. You saw how tough it was to get the dogs ready today," she reminded them. "It would have been really hard without you two."

"It didn't feel like work to us," Mandy said. "Today was the best day we've had in ages!"

"In that case, how about coming around for the next run on Monday morning?" suggested Hannah.

James looked gloomy. "I wish we could. But we have school."

"Oh, of course," said Hannah.

"But if the snow keeps up, school might be closed," Mandy said hopefully. "And if that happens, we'll definitely come. Won't we, James?"

He nodded. "Even if we have to wear snowshoes to get here."

"Or get Blackie to pull us in your toboggan," Mandy teased.

But to Mandy's disappointment, there was school as usual on Monday. Even though the fields were still covered in thick snow, the roads were clear and the bus had no trouble getting to Walton. Still, she had something to look forward to when she got home that afternoon. Teal, the young ferret, was coming in for his distemper vaccination.

Mandy raced home from the bus stop and arrived just as Steve took Teal into Dr. Emily's treatment room.

"He is so cute," Mandy said enthusiastically. She stood on one side of the examination table, stroking the little blue-gray creature to keep him calm. Her mom was checking him to make sure he was well enough to have the injection.

Teal twitched his nose. He seemed a little nervous at

finding himself in a strange place filled with the scents of other animals. Suddenly, he sneezed.

"Bless you!" Mandy said.

Teal sneezed again and his eyes began to water.

Dr. Emily frowned. "Has he been sneezing much?"

"To be honest, I don't know," replied Steve, who was watching anxiously. "I've been very busy on the farm so I haven't been able to spend a lot of time with him. But he did sneeze once or twice on the way here."

"And how is his appetite?" she asked.

"Well, he didn't seem too hungry this morning," Steve admitted.

Dr. Emily took out a thermometer. "Let's see what his temperature is."

It was 103.1°F — higher than normal.

"Does that mean he can't have his shot today?" said Mandy. She knew that a high temperature, though not necessarily serious, meant that Teal might not be well enough to be vaccinated.

Dr. Emily shook her head. "I'm afraid it's worse than that. It might be too late for the injection."

Mandy felt her heart plummet. "Too late?" she echoed, already guessing what her mom was going to say.

"Yes," said Dr. Emily. "I think Teal might already have distemper."

Seven

"He *can't* have distemper!" Mandy gasped. "He's only a baby."

Steve looked horrified. "It's not possible. Fizz and Charm have been vaccinated, and there aren't any unvaccinated dogs on the farm. Where on earth would Teal have picked up the virus?"

"Probably where he came from," said Dr. Emily. "Where did you get him?"

"From a man I met at the inn," said Steve.

Dr. Emily raised her eyebrows, so Steve hastily added, "Fred Jones has lots of ferrets, but he looks after them properly. I checked before I bought Teal. I even saw the

73

vaccination certificates for Fred's other ferrets." He
shook his head again. "Teal couldn't have picked it up
from them."

"Actually, he could have," Dr. Emily said grimly.

Mandy frowned. "But if the others have all been vaccinated, surely they can't get distemper or even pass
it on?"

"Well, there have been a few cases recently of ferrets
being given the wrong vaccine — a type that's really
meant for dogs, but if a ferret is injected with it by mis-
take, it can get distemper," said Dr. Emily. "It's really
unlucky, and vets are becoming much more aware
of the problem, but one or two cases have slipped
through."

"Poor Teal," Mandy said, running her fingers through
the soft fur on his back. "Is distemper as bad for a ferret as it is for a dog?" she asked her mom. She knew
that dogs who got the disease had a really bad time.
Their nervous systems were affected so that they trem-
bled uncontrollably, and many of them ended up with
pneumonia. Even if a dog survived, it might never fully
recover.

"Just as bad," said Dr. Emily.

"So what do we do now?" asked Steve.

Dr. Emily looked kindly at him. "Let's not jump to con-
clusions. We don't know for sure that it *is* distemper.

We'll keep Teal here for a few days to do some tests." She put her hand on Steve's arm. "At least you know that if Teal does have distemper, Fizz and Charm will be OK because their shots are up-to-date. Adam and I check all our vaccinations to make sure they're the right ones for ferrets."

Steve picked up Teal and held him close to his chest. "I'll come and visit you as soon as I can. You'll be fine, little guy." He handed Teal back to Mandy then left, taking Teal's basket with him. The empty wicker container seemed to emphasize just how serious things were.

"Should I take Teal to the residential unit now?" Mandy asked.

"Actually, he'll have to be kept in isolation," said her mom. "The annex is empty at the moment so we can put him in there." The annex was separate from the residential unit so that wild animals could be kept apart from domestic animals to prevent cross-infection.

"It's good we have a separate area," Mandy observed. "It would be terrible if other pets came here to get better and ended up with distemper."

"Quiver's puppies included," remarked Dr. Emily, wiping down the examination table with a strong disinfectant. "I'm afraid you won't be able to visit the puppies again, Mandy. Not for a few weeks, at least."

Mandy stared at her mom in dismay. "What?"

Dr. Emily stroked the ferret's tiny head. "If Teal does have distemper, there's a risk that you could carry it to the puppies. They can't be vaccinated until they're older."

This was *really* bad news. It meant Mandy would miss out on all the puppies' early milestones — when they opened their eyes, when they started to run and play, the first signs of their individual personalities! But then Mandy thought of the alternative: the chance that the five adorable puppies could contract a deadly virus.

"I just hope I haven't already passed it on to them," she said, feeling a shiver of fear.

"It's unlikely," said Dr. Emily. "Teal wouldn't have had the virus long before the symptoms started to show." She put her arm around Mandy's shoulder. "I know how much those huskies mean to you. You can phone Hannah every day for an update." Mandy nodded.

They took Teal to the annex and settled him inside a cozy cage that usually accommodated wild creatures like orphaned baby foxes or injured owls. Teal looked around nervously and sneezed again. His symptoms seemed to be getting worse.

Mandy was close to tears. "It's all right, Teal," she whispered, stroking his silky coat. "We're going to take care of you." But more than that, she couldn't promise.

*   *   *

The next morning, Mandy went to check on Teal before going to school. He stared out miserably from his cage, his eyes and nose running.

"Poor, poor Teal," she murmured. "Mom will be here in a minute. I'm sure she'll give you something to make you feel better." But there probably wasn't a lot that Dr. Emily could do for him right now. Apart from vaccinations, there was little that could be done to treat viral diseases.

Mandy heard the click of the door and she looked up, expecting to see her mom. But it was James.

"Ready?" he asked, putting his head around the door. Mr. Hunter was going to Walton this morning so he was giving Mandy and James a ride to school.

"Just about," Mandy said. "See you later, Teal." She smoothed the ferret's velvety fur once more.

"Teal? Is that Steve Barker's ferret?" said James. He pushed open the door and came in.

"Wait!" Mandy began but it was too late. James had reached Teal's cage and was peering in.

"You're going to wish you hadn't done that." Mandy warned. "Now you won't be able to visit the puppies, either."

James frowned. "What do you mean?"

"Teal might have distemper," Mandy explained. "We could pass it to the puppies if we have any contact with them."

"Well, I wouldn't have gone without you," James said loyally.

Teal sneezed again, and James looked closely at the young ferret. "You do look sick," he commented. "You look like you've got a cold, like me," he added, taking out a handkerchief to blow his nose.

"I thought you sounded a bit stuffed up," Mandy remarked.

James tried to say something, but a fit of sneezing stopped him.

"What's this? Another patient?" It was Dr. Emily, coming in to look at Teal.

James nodded and took off his glasses to wipe his eyes. Mandy felt a stab of sympathy for him; his nose looked very red and his eyes were watery.

"At least James only has a cold," Mandy commented. "Even if his symptoms are exactly the same as Teal's!"

Dr. Emily pushed a strand of hair out of her face and smiled. "You know, you might just have something there."

"What do you mean?"

"It's absolutely possible that James and Teal are suffering from the same thing!" Dr. Emily replied.

James's eyes widened. "You mean I've got distemper, too?"

"No, no!" Dr. Emily put her arm around James's shoulders to reassure him. "What I mean is that, like you, Teal might just have an ordinary cold."

"Can ferrets get colds?" Mandy asked in surprise.

"Yep," said Dr. Emily. "Often from humans, in fact."

"That's it!" Mandy gasped, suddenly remembering the first time she'd met Teal. It was the day she and her dad had seen Mr. Matthews. The farmer had been sneezing a lot — from a bad cold! "Teal could have picked up a cold from Mr. Matthews!"

"We don't know that for sure," Dr. Emily warned. "But I can do some tests right now."

"How long before you know?" Mandy asked.

"About ten minutes. Fifteen, maybe."

Mandy looked at her watch. There was only a half hour to go before school started, and Mr. Hunter was waiting for them in the car. But she'd never be able to concentrate in her classes if she didn't know Teal's results. "You don't think I could stay . . ."

"No, I don't think you could stay at home today," Dr. Emily interrupted. "Off you go, both of you."

"I'm sure Dad won't mind waiting a bit. I'll ask him," said James, hurrying out.

Dr. Emily lifted Teal out of his cage. "You go with James," she said to Mandy, "in case his dad can't wait."

Luckily, James's dad *could* wait. "But no more than ten minutes," he told Mandy and James.

"I'll make you a cup of tea," Mandy offered, hoping that it would take longer than ten minutes for her to make it and for Mr. Hunter to drink it. "Come inside where it's warm."

In the kitchen, she gave James's dad the newspaper, then put the kettle on the stove. She kept one eye on the door, hoping to see her mom coming in. There was so much hinging on the diagnosis: Teal's future, visits to the puppies, helping Hannah with the dogs, being involved with the Iditarod training. If it was nothing more than a cold, Mandy and James could keep visiting Black Tor Cottage, and best of all, Teal would get better.

After the kettle had boiled, Mandy was putting tea bags into the teapot when Simon, the clinic's nurse, came in. "Latest news flash," he said, and Mandy bit her lip.

"Teal is suffering from . . ."

James sucked in his breath.

". . . nothing more serious than the common cold," Simon finished.

"Yes!" Mandy jumped up, spun around, and hugged James who pulled away from her and said, "OK, OK. You're squishing me!"

"Isn't it the *best* news?" Mandy declared.

Mr. Hunter looked up from the newspaper. "Good news? About the weather? You've got to be joking!"

Puzzled, Mandy glanced at him and noticed the headline on the front page: MORE SNOW PREDICTED.

"That's great news, too!" Mandy exclaimed, and Mr. Hunter raised his eyebrows as if he thought she was crazy.

To Mandy's delight, it snowed so heavily overnight that school was closed the next day. Even though most of the roads around Welford were snowbound, she was determined to spend the day at Black Tor Cottage. She made two phone calls before breakfast: one to James to discuss how they could get there, and the second to Hannah, to say they'd be there later on to help out if she wanted them to.

"I could always use your help," said Hannah. "You're a fine pair of handlers. And all this snow means we're in for a good training run later today. But how will you get here? The road's terrible."

"We'll get there," Mandy said, sounding determined. She and James had decided that if it came to it, they'd walk. "A little deep snow won't hurt us," James had said on the phone. But then he'd sneezed, and Mandy had wondered if a walk through deep snow was a good idea for someone with a bad cold!

"I can give you a lift," said Dr. Adam, overhearing Mandy talking to Hannah. He eased a poached egg out of a saucepan with a spatula and put it on a plate. "You're in luck. I'm going up to see some sheep with foot trouble at Dyer's farm on the other side of the Tor, and I just bought a new set of tire chains yesterday for the Land Rover!"

Mandy would have hugged her dad if he weren't carrying a plate with a slippery poached egg. "Thanks, Dad," she said, beaming. "You're not just one of the best vets in the world. You're the best dad, too!"

Dr. Adam grinned. "Flattery will get you everywhere. Even to a remote Yorkshire cottage." He put the egg down in front of Dr. Emily.

"Thanks, Adam. That looks great."

"Is that all?" he teased. "I mean, doesn't a perfectly poached egg make me the best husband in the world, too?"

Dr. Emily gave him a wry smile. "Oh, absolutely — which makes me wonder what sort of fabulous surprises I can expect for Valentine's Day!"

Mandy jumped. In all the anxiety over Quiver, and then Teal, she had barely given a thought to Valentine's Day. It was just three days away! Three short days to Hannah and Michael's wedding, and less than a week before the couple and their twelve sled dogs left for Alaska.

An hour later, Dr. Adam dropped Mandy and James off at the cottage. Even before Mandy saw the huskies, she heard their energetic chorus blasting out from the kennels, the high-pitched yelps and howls of a team of sled dogs all fired up to run.

Hannah took Mandy and James out to the kennel area. Michael was already there, stretching the gang line out in the snow.

"Everything's ready!" he said, smiling at Hannah across the sled.

"Thanks, honey." She smiled back. "Could you harness Cindy for me please, James?" she said. "And Mandy, you can get Dart ready."

"Right-o," Mandy said.

Dart sprang to his paws as soon as he saw Mandy.

"Yes, you're going for a run." She laughed and smoothed his neck to calm him down before she slipped the harness over his shoulders.

"You're so good with the dogs, Mandy," said Hannah, watching her fasten the harness securely around Dart's middle. "You'll make a great musher one day."

Mandy beamed. "If I weren't going to be a vet, I might just think of going into dogsled racing," she said. She led Dart out. "Are they running in the same positions?" she double checked with Hannah, who was walking behind her with Dakota.

"We'll move them around today," she replied. "They need to be able to run in any position in case a dog is injured during the race. Keira and Odin can be the wheel dogs today, Cindy and Malik can be the team dogs, and these two" — she nodded at Dakota and Dart — "will run in the swing position." She clipped the neck line to Dakota's collar. "Of course, Leo's the only one who doesn't change places," she added as Michael came out with the big lead dog and took him to the head of the gang line.

"I can't imagine a better leader than Leo," Mandy said, positioning Dart alongside Dakota. "He's a real professional!" Leo strained against his harness, waiting for the signal to run.

"That's a good way to describe him," Michael agreed. He put an arm around Hannah and kissed the top of her head. "It's all thanks to Hannah — she's done all the hard work training him."

Hannah looked a little embarrassed. "Nonsense. You've done your part, too. Anyway, Leo's a natural leader."

James brought Cindy out and hitched her up without too much trouble. Michael noticed that a section of the gang line needed some adjustment then, so while he and Hannah fixed it, Mandy and James got the remaining dogs.

Malik seemed very restless, howling and pacing back and forth in his pen. "OK, OK. It's your turn now," said James.

Keira and Odin were excited, too, but not quite as worked up as Malik. "I think I should be able to manage both of you together," Mandy decided. But she'd underestimated Odin. As soon as he felt his harness go on, he started to leap around like a wild pony.

"Cool it, boy!" Mandy urged, but Odin kept jumping around, tugging Mandy from one side of the kennel to the other.

"Need some help?" James offered, even though he was struggling to keep a hold on Malik.

"Maybe he'll calm down in a minute," Mandy said. She managed to loop Odin's leash around the post in front of Keira's pen. "Wait here a second while I get Keira out," she told him.

But Odin obviously wasn't in the mood to wait. He leaped and snatched at his harness until Mandy was afraid he would break it. Inside the pen, Keira watched him with her head cocked to one side. She looked up at Mandy, her eyes vaguely puzzled as if she couldn't understand why her kennel-mate was causing such a fuss. She stood still while Mandy fastened the harness and collar, then trotted obediently out of the kennel with her.

"Odin, do you think you could cooperate, too?" Mandy sighed, unhitching his leash. She braced herself, waiting for him to rush off. Instead, he glanced at Keira and matched her pace exactly to walk obediently next to Mandy. When Mandy looked over her shoulder to see how James was doing, she saw that Malik had calmed down, too. Although he was still in a hurry and James had to walk fast to keep up with him, he wasn't pulling him around like before.

"Whatever you said to Odin worked on Malik, too." James grinned.

"I don't think it had anything to do with me," Mandy said. "Keira must have said something in Dog-lish."

Hearing her name, the young husky looked up at Mandy and blinked.

"Thanks for calming them down," Mandy said, running her hand over Keira's smooth head as they came into the yard.

"She seems to have that effect on all the dogs," said Michael, overhearing. He took Odin from Mandy and hitched him to the main line.

While Mandy put Keira into her place next to Odin, Hannah and James hitched up Malik. When the team was ready to go, Michael stood on the runners at the back of the sled.

"Are you the musher today?" James asked.

"For a while," answered Michael, pulling up the hood of his jacket. "We're doing a longer run today, and Hannah's a little tired. . . ." He looked at her with concern. She was leaning against the shed and yawning. "She'll take over when we're halfway up to the Tor." He pointed to a jagged black peak rising out of the snow. "The dogs should have settled down by then and will be easier to handle." He looked at James. "Can you release the snap line now?"

"Sure!" said James, and he flicked the quick-release on the line.

The line snapped, freeing the sled at the same time that Michael cried, "Hike up!" Like an arrow shot from a bow, the team burst through the gate. There was a breath-holding moment when the sled banged hard against one of the wooden posts and tipped over on one runner. Michael quickly leaned the other way to straighten it again.

"Careful!" yelled Hannah. "And keep on the path, Michael!" She suddenly looked at Mandy and James and made a face. "I forgot the dogs' booties!" She shook her head impatiently. "Too late now," she said.

Crunching through the thick powdery snow, they jogged after the sled. Even though they ran in the freshly made tracks, it was hard work, especially when the path sloped uphill.

Soon, they came to a stone post sticking out of the snow. "Black Tor, three miles," James read, looking rather red in the face. He sneezed and took out a hand-kerchief to blow his nose. "That's a long way to jog uphill."

"Not for the dogs," said Hannah.

The team was running at a steady pace about three hundred yards ahead. Mandy was just thinking how awesome they looked when a loud yelp rang out across the field, and the lead dog crashed to the ground.

"Leo's gone down!" she cried.

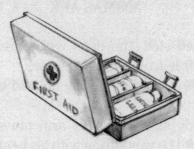

Eight

The other dogs couldn't stop in time. They thundered into Leo, bumping into one another and falling on top of their leader in a surging, yelping heap. Behind them, the sled jerked wildly. The back end tipped up and Michael was thrown off into the snow. Mandy heard him cry out once before his voice was drowned by the howling of the dogs.

Three hundred yards suddenly seemed like three hundred miles as Mandy charged up the track with James and Hannah. She could barely see Michael lying facedown in the snow, not moving. On the other side of the overturned sled, the dogs writhed and clamored, trying to get free from their harnesses.

Let them be OK, she silently begged over and over again.

Then Mandy saw Michael's arm move. He pushed himself up until he was sitting with his head in his hands, and Mandy breathed a sigh of relief.

But the dogs were still very distressed, snapping at one another and struggling wildly. Afraid that they might hurt themselves or each other, Mandy ran faster, finding an extra burst of energy.

Hannah fell onto her knees in the snow next to Michael and gently shook his arm. Mandy and James went straight to the dogs to calm them down. "It looks like some of the lines are tangled," Mandy said. "We'll have to unravel them."

Behind her, she heard Hannah talking to Michael. "Are you all right?"

"I think so," came the reply.

"What happened?" Hannah prompted.

Mandy and James were trying to separate Dakota and Cindy, whose lines were virtually braided together. The pair must have rolled over each other several times to get into such a tangle. Mandy released Dakota from the tug line first and held on to her harness while James tried to keep Cindy still so that he could untwist the lines.

"Something ran across the path," Mandy heard Michael explain. "I think it might have been a rabbit." She glanced over her shoulder and saw him rub his forehead as if he were trying to think more clearly.

"Dart pulled out to go after it," continued Michael, "then Leo —" He broke off. "The dogs! I've got to see to them." He stood up unsteadily.

"It's OK. We're here," Mandy called.

But Michael shook his head and kept walking, even though he looked as if he might fall down at any moment. He went to calm Odin first. The husky was straining against the tug line as if he was trying to run off.

"I'll check on Dart," said Hannah.

He was jumping and twisting like a fish on the line, unsettling Malik.

"That's enough, Dart!" Hannah said firmly. She gripped his harness to keep him still.

Behind them, James tried to settle Malik. "Easy, boy. Easy," he kept repeating.

Only two of the dogs weren't in a panic: Keira, who sat quietly in her place as if she knew the best thing to do was stay still and Leo, who lay on his side, panting heavily.

When Dakota had calmed down, Mandy checked that Keira was OK and then went over to Leo. She knelt next to him and smoothed her hand over his shoulder. "Ready to get up, big guy?" she said. She guessed he might have been winded by the fall; he wasn't tangled up because his lines were straight and still attached to the gang line correctly.

Leo lifted his head and blinked at her. Obediently, he began to get up. But as soon as he put his weight on his paws, he yelped and flopped down again.

"Leo's hurt!" Mandy exclaimed.

Hannah raced over and sat down next to Leo in the snow. She ran her hands down Leo's legs. "There's nothing obvious, like a cut," she said.

"Maybe he pulled a muscle," Mandy suggested.

"Or he could have tripped over that big stone," said James, pointing out a jagged rock half hidden by snow.

"That's probably it," Hannah agreed. "What bad luck!" She looked around, frowning. "Wait a minute — they weren't even on the path!" She said, pointing to a post marking the track about ten yards away.

Michael stumbled up and kneeled on the other side of Mandy. "I told you. Dart pulled out to the side when that rabbit shot across the path. The others must have changed direction, too."

"Well, you should have corrected them," Hannah said sharply.

"You know that's easier said than done," countered Michael.

"Maybe." Hannah sounded unconvinced. She lifted one of Leo's front legs to have a closer look at his foot.

Mandy leaned forward to look, too. "Some of his nails have been ripped out!" she exclaimed in horror. There were raw gashes at the ends of Leo's paws where the nails had come out, and clumps of frozen blood crusting the fur around his toes.

Leo whined and pulled his foot away.

"Ouch!" said James sympathetically. "That must hurt like crazy."

Hannah looked appalled. "If only I'd put booties on the dogs!"

"Don't blame yourself," said Michael. "Accidents like this can happen to anyone."

Hannah glared at him. "It wouldn't have happened if you'd kept on the path, and if you'd clipped Leo's nails. Look how long they are!" She pointed to the nails on the other front paw. "No wonder they got ripped out."

Michael's expression darkened. "Don't lay all the blame on me, Hannah. You could just as easily have clipped his nails."

"Oh, yes? When?"

"In the time you've wasted blaming me for everything that's gone wrong," retorted Michael.

Mandy felt uncomfortable. She stole a glance at

James who was concentrating very hard on something in the snow.

"I'll just see if all the others are still OK," Mandy mumbled. She headed for the back of the line and crouched down to take a look at Keira. The quiet husky nuzzled Mandy's hand in greeting. But she kept glancing unhappily at her owners as their heated argument continued.

"All I ask is that you do your part," Hannah was saying angrily to her fiancé.

Keira whimpered and looked up at Mandy. "It's all right," Mandy soothed. She took off her glove and stroked Keira's head. She wanted to say something to help the sensitive dog understand that her owners wouldn't be angry with each other forever. But she knew there was nothing she could do to make Keira feel better. She kneeled down and hugged her instead. The husky seemed to melt in her arms. She leaned into Mandy and licked her neck.

"That's a good girl," Mandy whispered. "Everything's going to be fine."

James came over, looking rather flustered. "Let's straighten up the sled," he suggested.

"Good idea." Mandy stood up. "I'll be back in a minute, Keira."

Being careful not to disturb the dogs, they heaved the sled over until it was on its runners again.

At the other end of the line of dogs, the fight was still going on. "Nothing I do is good enough!" Michael protested. "I'm beginning to wonder if there's any point in going ahead with the wedding."

"The wedding is the least of my worries!" Hannah shot back, her voice ringing out across the silent snowy field. "There isn't even going to be a race now that we don't have a lead dog."

No race! Mandy was horrified. After all the months of preparation, there wasn't going to be a race?

"They *can't* call it off," James whispered in disbelief.

"It'll take months to train another lead dog!" Hannah continued.

"We can't think about that now," Michael said. "Leo's paw needs attention. We've got to get him back to the house."

"I could run back and call my dad," Mandy offered shyly. "He might be able to drive the Land Rover up here."

"There isn't any access to this part of the field from the road," said Michael.

"We could pull Leo back on the sled," said James.

Hannah was kneeling next to Leo, holding his injured

paw in her hands. She looked at the sled, then at Leo. "It's our only option," she agreed. "We need to put a bandage on this paw first, but I don't have a first-aid kit with me." She glared at Michael. "I didn't think we'd need one on such a short training run."

"I've got a clean handkerchief," offered James. He took it out of his pocket. "Will this help?"

"It will until we get back to the house," said Hannah, taking it from him. "Thanks, James." She shook the handkerchief to unfold it, then tried to wrap it around Leo's paw. But Leo kept pulling his paw away. It must have been throbbing badly, and he didn't want anyone touching it.

"I'm trying to help you, Leo!" said Hannah in exasperation.

"I'll hold his leg still," Mandy said. Crouching down next to the dog, she held his foreleg firmly in both hands.

"Thanks, Mandy," said Hannah, folding the white handkerchief around Leo's paw. She brought two sides together and tied them in a knot. "Let's load him onto the sled."

Michael slid his arms beneath the dog and lifted him up. Leo looked rather surprised and struggled for a moment.

"Careful," said Hannah.

"I won't drop him, if that's what you mean," said

Michael a little impatiently. Holding Leo against his chest as if he were cradling a baby, he lowered him into the cargo bed.

Mandy and the others unhitched the rest of the dogs from the gang line. Their leashes were stowed on the sled, and they hooked the dogs to the harnesses. But when Mandy unhitched Keira, she discovered that they were one leash short.

"I must have dropped it in the field," said Hannah. She looked at Keira standing patiently beside Mandy. "But I don't think Keira's going to give us any trouble. There seems to be quite a bond between you two."

Despite her worries about Leo, Mandy felt a sense of

pride. She'd grown very fond of Keira and it was reward-ing to know that the feeling was mutual.

With Michael in the lead, but walking behind the sled so that he could control it more easily, they set off down the hill. At first, the dogs were puzzled to see the sled in front of them. They whined and pulled on their leads, trying to catch up with it.

James leaned back to stop Cindy and Dart from tug-ging him over, while Hannah had to stop and make Malik and Dakota sit for a few moments to calm them down.

Mandy had an easier time. On her left, Keira trotted along obediently as if there was an invisible line linking the two of them. Once or twice, she nosed Mandy's hand affectionately and Mandy reached down to pat her silky head.

She had Odin on her right. At first, he tried to pull away. But then he glanced across at Keira and stopped tugging, dropping back to match her pace.

It took them nearly a half hour to get back to the cot-tage. Michael lifted Leo out of the cargo bed and carried him into the living room. James had offered to take care of the rest of the dogs so he stayed out in the ken-nel area.

Michael put Leo down on a rug. "Sorry, boy," he said, stroking Leo's head. "I really should have cut your nails."

Leo looked at Michael without a trace of resentment,

and when Michael put his arms around the big dog's neck to hug him, Leo nuzzled against him as if he'd already forgiven him.

Hannah came in with a bowl of warm water and disinfectant. "Keep his leg still for me please, Mandy, while I wash his paw," she said.

Mandy felt rather embarrassed. Hannah could easily have asked Michael to help because he was sitting next to Leo. Obviously, she was still angry with him.

Michael stood up. "I'll get the first-aid kit," he said, going out of the room.

Outside, it sounded as if James had his hands full. A barrage of yelps and howls came from the kennel, punctuated by James crying out "Down, boy!" or "No! This way, Odin."

Michael returned with the first-aid kit. "I'll bandage Leo's paw," he offered.

"No," Hannah said bluntly. "I'll do it."

Michael frowned. "Have it your way." He dropped the bandage on the floor next to Hannah, and Mandy winced.

Out in the kennel, James was yelling, "Dart! Come here!"

"I think James will appreciate my help more than you, Hannah," said Michael, and he strode out of the living room.

Mandy concentrated on patting Leo's paw dry with a clean towel. "Do you have any ointment?" she asked Hannah.

"There's a tube of antiseptic cream in here." Hannah rummaged around in the first-aid kit until she found the ointment and squeezed a dollop onto her finger. "Hold still a moment, Leo," she said, dabbing the cream onto his paw.

Leo didn't move. He must have understood that Hannah and Mandy were helping him. He lay with his head in Mandy's lap while Hannah bandaged his paw again. When she'd finished, he licked her cheek as if he were thanking her.

He's really attached to her, Mandy thought. *And to Michael. I hope they make up soon.*

Mandy stayed with Leo while Hannah went to make some warm drinks. Outside, the yelps had stopped so she guessed that Michael had managed to get things under control. She wondered how Keira was. *I hope Michael's reassured her that everything's OK.*

A few minutes later, James came in looking quite disheveled. There was a creak on the floorboards above, and Mandy guessed Michael had gone straight upstairs.

"Remind me never to have more than one dog." James grinned.

"Tough time?" Mandy asked sympathetically.

"You can say that again. They're amazing dogs, but they're a real handful," said James. He took off his glasses to remove some dog hair that was stuck to them. "But Michael's great with them. They really listen to him."

"And I think he loves them just as much as Hannah does," Mandy said. "How's Keira?"

"She's still a little upset. We gave her some food, but she didn't want it."

A movement at the door caught Mandy's eye. It was Michael with his car keys in hand.

A clatter of cups came from the kitchen, followed by Hannah's voice.

"Going somewhere?" She sounded more tense than ever.

"There's no point in me being here," said Michael, with an edge of anger to his voice. "I don't even know if there is a point to us anymore."

"Does that mean the wedding's off?" James whispered to Mandy.

"It can't be!" Mandy whispered back. She hated listening to grown-ups arguing, especially about personal things like their relationships. She looked at her watch, wishing her dad would arrive to pick them up.

"And what about the dogs?" Hannah demanded. "How do you expect me to take care of them by myself?"

After a slight pause, Michael said, "Isn't it a little late to think about that now? I mean, you've always acted like you're the only one who can do it right."

"You know that's not true!" Hannah sounded close to tears.

"No, I don't. You criticize *everything* I do," argued Michael. "But because I *do* care about the dogs, I'll come over when I'm not at work to feed and groom them. You won't need my help with training sessions. No lead dog means no race, remember?"

Hannah said nothing. Moments later, Mandy heard the front door open and then bang shut.

"Wow!" whispered James. "He really means it."

Hannah came into the living room then with mugs of cocoa and tea and a bowl of water on a tray. "Sorry it took so long," she said, sounding choked up. She offered the water to Leo, who lapped it up thirstily before resting his head on Mandy's lap again.

Hannah sipped her tea. "The pups could do with some food," she said, putting down her mug. "I'm still giving them a bottle every day to make things easier for Quiver. Anyone want to help?"

"Sure," said Mandy. She eased Leo's head off her lap. "See you later," she told him.

In the puppy room, the little huskies were sound asleep.

"Hi, guys," Mandy said, kneeling down next to the whelping box. Hearing her voice, Nemo stretched and looked straight at her with bright blue eyes.

"His eyes are open!" she exclaimed. Four more sets of blue eyes blinked at her. "Of course," Mandy said, counting the days in her head. "They're eleven days old now."

"Oh, I should have told you their eyes had opened," said Hannah. "But in all the . . ." she trailed off.

"Yes, it's been a busy day," Mandy said carefully. She took one of the bottles and picked up Nemo to feed him.

The little white husky drained the bottle in less than a minute.

"Keep up that appetite and you'll end up bigger than your brothers and sisters." Mandy chuckled, pulling the bottle out of his mouth. She returned him to the whelping box and he snuggled up next to his mother.

Hannah bent over the box and ran her finger down Nemo's back. Suddenly, she looked up and smiled at Mandy. "The puppies are doing so well now. I couldn't have wished for a better litter."

Mandy was delighted to see her face light up after such a horrible morning. There was nothing like a gorgeous animal to cheer people up!

Nine

Baby ferrets were pretty good for making people smile, too. When Mandy climbed into her dad's Land Rover after he'd arrived to pick up her and James, she saw a tiny face peeping out from a cage on the front seat.

"Teal!" she exclaimed. "What are you doing here?" She put her hand against the cage, and Teal sniffed it through the wire.

"He's much better. No more sneezing or watery eyes," Dr. Adam told her. He started up the engine. "I thought we'd drop him off at Burnside Farm. We'll give him a few days at home to get his strength back, then we'll give him his distemper shot."

"Won't he give his cold to the other ferrets?" said James.

"I doubt it," said Dr. Adam.

"It's nice to have some good news for a change," James said, sighing.

"Yes, it's very unfortunate about Leo," agreed Dr. Adam. He'd examined Leo's paw and was satisfied that Hannah and Mandy had done a good job. But Leo would have to be kept quiet for a few days, and he certainly wouldn't be able to run for several weeks.

The husky team no longer had a leader. For Hannah, the Iditarod was over. Just thinking about it as they drove down the hill made Mandy feel depressed all over again. "I can't believe everything's turned out so badly," she murmured.

When they reached Burnside Farm, Steve came out to meet them.

Mandy got out of the Land Rover and handed the cage to him. "Special delivery," she declared. "One baby ferret in perfect condition."

"Great!" Steve exclaimed. "We missed you, little guy! Come and see what I made for you."

Inside the house, he proudly showed them a brand-new cage he'd just finished. It was very big with lots of features designed to keep Teal busy, including tunnels and wheels and branches for climbing. There was also a cozy sleeping area that resembled a little cave.

"That's got to be the most luxurious ferret home in the world!" said James.

"Yes, I wouldn't mind moving in there myself." Lisa laughed. She was sitting on the floor with Fizz and Charm snuggled up on her lap like a pair of cats.

Steve raised his eyebrows in mock indignation. "If that's a dig at me for not decorating the bedroom, then it worked. I'll start on it first thing in the morning."

Lisa grinned happily.

Mandy couldn't help comparing the cheerful banter between this couple with the hurtful exchanges between Hannah and Michael. Steve and Lisa's pets seemed to bring them closer together. But Hannah and Michael couldn't seem to agree on anything as far as their huskies were concerned. And it wasn't only the humans who felt unhappy. Mandy was worried that the dogs could sense their masters' discomfort.

"What's in the package?" Mandy asked her mom when she arrived home.

Dr. Emily was sitting at the kitchen table, wrapping something in white-and-gold paper. "It's a wedding gift," she said. She unfolded the paper and held up two pairs of bright blue thermal long johns. "I know they're not exactly romantic, but I'm sure they'll be very useful when Hannah and Michael arrive in Alaska."

"They're not going anymore," Mandy said, slumping down in a chair. "The wedding's off."

"What do you mean?" gasped her mom.

Mandy put her elbows on the table and cupped her chin in her hands. "Michael and Hannah had another fight."

"Just wedding jitters, I expect," said Dr. Emily. She continued wrapping the long johns.

Mandy shook her head. "It's worse than that. Leo was hurt. He won't be able to race for ages." She told her mom about the accident. "So even if Hannah and Michael do make up, they won't be going to the Iditarod," she finished.

Dr. Adam came in from the garage. "Bad luck about Leo, hmm?" he said.

"Yes. It had to have been pretty rough for him, and painful, too. But surely Hannah can use one of her other dogs as the leader?" Dr. Emily suggested.

Mandy shook her head. "I don't think any of the other dogs could do it. It took Hannah years to train Leo. She'd have said if another dog could take his place."

Dr. Adam filled the kettle with water. "She might not have trained another one as leader, but there *could* be a potential leader among the pack."

Mandy frowned. "What do you mean?"

"People say leaders are born, not made," her dad

answered. He took a teapot out of a cabinet and dropped a few tea bags into it.

"It's the same with pack animals like dogs," Dr. Emily said. "If a dog has the mental ability — the right instincts, really — he can successfully lead a pack."

This made sense to Mandy. "I guess we're looking for a dog that's strong-willed and very confident," she said. She pictured all the dogs in Hannah's kennels. "Dart? No." He was much too impulsive, especially when it came to things like rabbits! "Odin's quite an independent character," she said. "He knows what he wants, so he might be a good choice. And Bayonet looks tough enough to lead a team. Malik, too. He's got a strong nature and he's very outgoing."

Dr. Emily looked thoughtful. "A good leader isn't necessarily physically strong or forceful. A calm, clear-thinking dog might be a better bet than one that's very independent."

Mandy frowned. "You can't have a weak, timid dog in front."

"Not timid, I agree," said her mom. "But when you think about it, the real leader of the team is the musher. A dominant dog in front might not be willing to listen to all the commands."

"But a lead dog has to sort of guide all the others," Mandy insisted.

"Yes, but in response to the musher's commands," said Dr. Adam, pouring boiling water into the teapot. "What your mom's saying is that a quieter, calmer dog is probably better in front than one that's a little too big for its boots."

"So a calm dog that cooperates with the musher," Mandy said slowly.

Dr. Adam stirred the tea. "That's about right. Know anyone who fits the bill?"

"I think so," Mandy said. A picture filled her mind of a gentle, dusky gray dog with sapphire-blue eyes. "Keira! She's calm, sensitive, and definitely has the respect of the others. Even Odin takes his lead from her." She pushed her chair back. "I have to tell Hannah!"

But Dr. Emily stopped her. "Don't interfere, Mandy. Hannah needs to figure things out for herself. She knows her dogs better than anyone, and if she really wants to race, she'll come up with the solution."

Mandy sat down again, feeling frustrated.

"Anyway, it sounds like Hannah has other matters on her mind right now," her mom continued. "Like making up with Michael before Saturday. I'm sure they'll be fine once they've had a good heart-to-heart."

Mandy wished she shared her mom's confidence. After seeing how angry Hannah and Michael were with

each other after the sled accident, she didn't think there
was any chance at all that the wedding would go on.

There was more heavy snowfall overnight, so Mandy's
school was still closed the next day. Because of the bad
weather, it was also very quiet at Animal Ark. Few people brought their pets in, and there were no patients in
the residential unit.

After breakfast, Mandy picked up the remote and
flicked through the channels on television but there was
nothing worth watching, so she turned the television
off and picked up a book. But her mind was so full of
Hannah and Michael and the huskies, she couldn't concentrate. She tossed the book onto the coffee table and
went to look out the window.

The snow-covered landscape just made her think of
Alaska and the Iditarod. If only Hannah would realize
that Keira could probably take over!

"Penny for your thoughts."

Mandy jumped. "Dad! You scared me."

"Sorry," he said. "You looked a million miles away."

"Not that far." She managed to smile. "Only Alaska."

"And Black Tor Cottage, I bet. I'm going up to check on
Leo this afternoon. I could do with some company. But if
you've got something better to do, I'll understand."

Mandy gave him a playful shove. "Of course I've got

tons of more important things to do," she joked. "Like shoveling snow off the driveway."

"Now, that's not a bad idea," said her dad.

"OK. I'll just call James to see if he wants to come with us this afternoon."

But James's cold had gotten much worse. "I can hardly breathe," he complained stuffily. "And I can't stop coughing. Mom says I have to stay in bed."

"Poor you," Mandy sympathized. "I'll ask Dad to bring me over later so I can tell you how Leo is."

"Thanks," said James, before a bout of coughing interrupted him and he had to put down the phone.

"You're a very good dog," Mandy said, patting Leo while her dad examined his injured paw. After checking on Quiver and the pups, they'd come to the kennels to see Leo. As always, the huskies launched into earsplitting yelps when they appeared.

"You kept your bandage on all night," Mandy went on, speaking loudly to make herself heard. She thought Leo might have pulled the dressing off, because not many dogs were happy to have bandages on.

"He *is* a good dog, and very cooperative," Hannah agreed. She was looking pale, and Mandy noticed that her eyes were puffy as if she'd been crying. "That's what makes him such a good leader."

Here was Mandy's chance to suggest Keira for lead dog! "Speaking of leaders . . ." she began but then her dad's cell phone rang.

"Hi, Mr. Dyer. What can I do for you?" He listened for a moment. "A breech lambing? What luck! How's the road up to the farm?" Another pause, then, "Big drifts? Hmm." He frowned. "I think I'd better talk you through it over the phone."

Mandy and Hannah exchanged a puzzled look.

"Just one second," continued Dr. Adam. "I'll go somewhere quieter." He lowered the phone and said to Mandy and Hannah, "I'll be in the kitchen, talking Mr. Dyer through a breech lambing." He hurried out of the kennels.

Mandy tried to pick up the conversation again. "We were talking about lead dogs," she prompted.

"Hmm, leaders." Hannah had gone into Odin's enclosure and was checking his nails. She took a pair of nail clippers out of her pocket to trim the nails on his back paws.

"I wonder if Odin could ever become a leader?" Mandy pressed on, leaning over the gate.

"This self-contained, aloof character?" Hannah managed to smile. "It would be like putting a missile in front of the team!"

"So a leader should be focused on the other dogs

as well as the musher?" Mandy checked. "And be calm, too?"

"That pretty much sums up a lead dog," said Hannah. She picked up one of Odin's front paws to inspect it.

"So quiet dogs can make good leaders?"

Hannah put down Odin's paw. "Yes. A quiet, unruffled dog is a real asset to a team, especially in the lead." She looked impressed. "You certainly know a lot about dogs, don't you, Mandy?"

"A little. Mom and Dad know more, of course," Mandy acknowledged. "They explained how a dog needs the right instincts to be a good leader." She glanced at Keira's kennel, hoping she wasn't being too obvious.

"Are you thinking of Keira?"

Mandy nodded, unsure what to say next.

Hannah gave Odin a treat, then stood up. "Interesting," she said.

Mandy held her breath. She wanted Hannah to say something like "of course, Keira is the obvious answer! Why hadn't I thought about her before? Now we can go to Alaska after all!"

"Keira might have the potential to be a leader," Hannah went on, and something in her tone made Mandy's heart plummet, "but she's still very young and doesn't have half the experience of the other dogs." She

closed the gate to Odin's kennel and walked over to
Keira's enclosure, but stopped before she went in.
"Anyway, what's the point of even thinking about
another leader when there's not going to be a wedding,
a honeymoon, or a trip to Alaska?" With that, she burst
into tears.

Keira gazed at her owner with a mixture of curiosity
and gentle affection on her face. As Hannah buried her
face in her hands and sobbed, Keira's expression
changed to one of concern. She jumped up against the
wire, whimpering.

Mandy found herself fighting back her own tears.
Even though Keira was young, she seemed to understand so much. And there was a bond between the
husky and her owner that no amount of training could
ever achieve. *She's one of the most sensitive dogs
I've ever met*, Mandy thought.

Her instinct was to go over and comfort the dog, but
she stayed where she was, reluctant to interfere.

"Sorry," Hannah said, dabbing her eyes. Undoing the
bolt on the gate, she slipped into the pen.

Keira jumped up at Hannah. But not in an excited
way. Instead, it looked as if she were trying to comfort
her owner. Standing with her front paws on Hannah's
thighs, she looked anxiously up at her.

"Oh, Keira," sobbed Hannah. She bent down and put her arms around the dog's neck. "You're a treasure. You always know when someone's in trouble, don't you?"

Mandy felt like giving the gorgeous dog a big hug, too. But Hannah probably needed some privacy. *I'll go back into the house to see if Quiver needs to go for a walk*, she decided. She began to walk away but stopped dead when Hannah suddenly said, "This just won't work!"

She sounded angry again. Had she discovered something else that Michael hadn't done correctly? Something in Keira's kennel?

Hoping it wasn't anything too serious, Mandy looked back.

Hannah straightened up and pushed her hair out of her face. "I have to pull myself together. What kind of musher am I if I fall at the first hurdle? We've got to make the best of things, right?"

"Uh, I guess so," Mandy muttered awkwardly.

"And for a musher, a sled run is definitely the way to make the best of things," Hannah continued, coming out of the pen.

Mandy's heart skipped a beat. Was Keira about to get the chance to prove herself as a lead dog?

Hannah went over to where the harnesses hung on the wall. "Leo's the best lead dog I've ever had. But it's crazy to have only one trained leader — like having no spare tire for your car." She unhooked the harnesses. "Whether there's going to be a wedding or a race or nothing at all, it's time I started training a backup leader." Looking very determined, she handed Mandy some of the harnesses. "Mandy, you've made me see sense at last. Let's see if Keira really has it in her. Are you up for a run?"

"Definitely!" Mandy exclaimed.

As she slipped the harness over Keira's shoulders, she whispered, "You can do it, girl, I know you can! All you have to do is prove it to Hannah." And crossing her fingers, she led the apprentice leader outside.

Ten

Keira seemed surprised when Mandy attached her to the front of the gang line. She looked back at the other dogs, then tipped her head on one side as if she were asking Mandy what was going on.

"It's just like all the runs you've done before," Mandy told her, stroking her head. "You're in a different position, that's all. Indy's taken your old place."

Indy was a dog who Mandy had just met that morning — one of the regular breeding huskies. She hadn't been on many runs since her last litter of pups six months before. But with one dog short, this was an opportunity for Hannah to start building up Indy's fitness again.

Hannah had gone to the cottage to get jackets for herself and Mandy. She came out carrying a headlamp on a stretchy strap, too. "It'll be dark soon," she said. She switched on the lamp to make sure it was working.

"Don't the dogs mind running in the dark?" Mandy asked, putting on one of the parkas.

"No. If we'd gone to the Iditarod" — a tone of regret crept into Hannah's voice — "we'd have done most of the running at night. It's cooler then," she explained. She put the headlamp around her forehead and zipped up her parka. "Ready, Keira?" She crouched in front of the new leader and cupped her pretty face in her hands.

Keira wagged her tail and licked Hannah's cheek. *I'll give it my best shot*, she seemed to say.

"We'll do one loop of the field first. If all goes well, I'll come back for you, Mandy, and we'll go for a longer run," said Hannah, standing up again.

The team was as eager as ever to head out into the field. They panted and pawed restlessly at the ground. Keira was calmer than the others, though. She gazed patiently at Mandy as if she were waiting to take the command to go.

"I'm not your musher," Mandy chuckled. "I'm just here for the ride."

"Oh, no, you're not." Hannah grinned, stepping onto the runners. "You're my number one handler. And right now, I need you to free the sled."

Mandy released the snub line. At the same time, Hannah called, "Hike up!"

There was no explosive start like before. Keira looked around uncertainly while the rest of the team grew more restless. Some jerked on their neck lines. Others lunged forward and looked bewildered when their leader didn't move.

"Hike up, Keira!" Hannah called again.

Keira twisted around and seemed to frown at her owner.

"Go on, Keira!" Mandy whispered softly.

Keira either heard her, or sensed Mandy urging her on. She looked directly at Mandy and lifted her head. Hannah repeated the command and this time Keira set off at a trot. Behind her, the team matched her pace and the sled moved forward smoothly.

"Good girl!" called Hannah, then she winced as Keira turned too sharply going through the gate. The side of the sled hit the gatepost with a thud.

"Easy!" yelled Hannah.

Mandy held her breath as the sled bounced off the post. *Don't let it all go wrong now!* she thought.

Keira seemed rattled and her stride faltered.

"Straight on!" Hannah commanded, and Keira lengthened her stride.

Mandy ran to the gate to watch the team run across the snow. They weren't going as fast as when Leo had been in the lead. *But at least they're going along smoothly*, she told herself.

Hannah let the dogs run in a straight line for a few minutes before calling out a command. At first Keira didn't respond, and when Hannah called out again, the new leader wavered before veering to the right.

"No. Haw!" shouted Hannah so loudly that Mandy could hear her, too. She wondered if Keira understood the commands. After all, until today, she'd always simply followed Leo. She hadn't had to listen carefully to her musher.

But then she saw Keira correct herself and turn to the left. Mandy had underestimated her.

Ten minutes later, Hannah drew up alongside Mandy. "She made a few errors, but it wasn't bad for a first try," she said. Her eyes shone and her cheeks were flushed with excitement. "Are you ready for a ride?"

"You bet!" Mandy said. She climbed into the cargo bed, pulling her knees up against her chest and wrapping her arms around them. Now that the sun had gone down, it was getting really cold.

"Time for some light," said Hannah. She switched on

the headlamp. The beam cut through the dusk, casting a narrow yellow path onto the snow.

They swished smoothly across the field. This time, Keira seemed a lot more confident. She responded to nearly all Hannah's commands. Once, she turned right when she should have continued straight, and when Hannah called to her to slow down at one point, she went faster. But these were small mistakes.

"She's really good!" Mandy cried when Keira, on her own initiative, pulled out about ten yards from a big rock so that the others had time to avoid it, too.

"Not bad at all," Hannah agreed.

Suddenly, the beam from the headlamp fell on a rabbit. Startled, the creature shot off, zigzagging across the white field. Mandy braced herself. Would Dart be able to resist another chase?

"Straight on!" Hannah commanded in a very firm voice.

Mandy waited for Dart to leap to one side, but up ahead Keira glanced at the rabbit. She listened to Hannah's commands, keeping on the path and setting the pace. Behind her, in the swing position, Dart didn't misplace a foot. His focus remained on his leader and he pounded along as if the rabbit hadn't been there at all.

"Go, Keira!" Mandy whispered. She couldn't shout out because it would confuse the dogs, but inside her head she was turning cartwheels in triumph. The gentle husky was born to lead!

As they raced across the field, Mandy thought she heard a voice calling to them. She glanced back and spotted a figure waving to them from the gate. Hannah commanded Keira to turn and they headed back toward the yard.

Mandy's dad was waiting for them. "I don't know," he said, smiling when they pulled up. "I go into the kitchen for fifteen minutes, and when I come back, you two are heading for the Arctic in the pitch dark!"

"I wish we could have gone all the way to the Arctic!" Mandy felt herself bubbling over with excitement. "Keira's great, Dad! She got the hang of being lead dog in no time at all."

"I've gotta say, she looked pretty good from here," he said. "You must be very happy with her, Hannah."

"Oh, I am. A few more sessions and she'll be sound as a bell." Hannah stepped off the runners and walked alongside the sled as the dogs pulled it into the yard. "She reminds me a lot of a dog my dad bred, named Aurora. She was a quiet dog, too, but very wise."

Still sitting in the sled, Mandy felt a warm glow of satisfaction. She had been right!

She helped Hannah to unhitch the dogs, and Dr. Adam took them into the kennels to bed them down.

When Hannah came to Keira, she gave her new lead dog a warm hug. "You were superb. I just wish Michael had been here to see you."

There was a sound behind them then. Mandy, who was packing the gang line into the sled, thought it was her dad coming out of the kennels. She saw Keira look around and wag her tail.

Then a voice that wasn't her dad's said, "I *did* see her, actually."

"Michael!" exclaimed Hannah. She ran across the yard and into his arms. "I'm so sorry . . ." she began, but Michael pushed her away gently.

Mandy felt a wave of disappointment crash over her. It looked as if Michael didn't want to make up yet. She crouched down and put an arm around Keira's neck, to comfort the dog who was watching her owners intently.

"Hannah, listen," said Michael. He sounded so serious that Mandy held her breath.

Suddenly, he dropped onto one knee in the snow. Taking one of Hannah's hands into his own, he looked up at her and said, "Will you marry me? Please?"

"Oh!" was all Hannah could say.

A playful smile flickered across Michael's face. "Maybe on Saturday, in Welford Church?" he continued.

"Only if you have nothing better to do. Then I was thinking we could head off for a honeymoon in Alaska."

Hannah tried to speak but instead she burst into tears. She dropped onto her knees as well and gave Michael a huge hug. "Of course, I will." With her face buried in the collar of his coat, she whispered, "I'm sorry I let us come to this. It all just got to be too much for me, coping with Quiver and the wedding plans and training the dogs. I should never have taken it out on you, the one person who's supported me all along."

Michael stroked her hair. "It's all right, I understand. I could have handled things better, too. You don't need to worry about dealing with anything on your own now."

Mandy felt Keira trembling against her. The husky's ears pricked up and her sapphire eyes shone. Whining softly, she licked Mandy's face and tried to pull away from her.

"All right," Mandy said, understanding. She let Keira go and stepped back.

The new leader bounded forward and squirmed between her owners. Hannah laughed through her tears and wrapped her arms around the husky to pull her into the hug.

Dr. Adam came out of the kennels. "What's going on?" he whispered to Mandy.

"Let's just say that one of the dogs of war is really a husky with a heart," she said, beaming.

Dr. Adam looked even more confused.

Hannah straightened up. When Mandy saw the expression on her face, she caught her breath. Hannah was looking very troubled. Was she about to change her mind?

"There might be a problem," Hannah said. "I do want to marry you, Michael, I promise, but very heavy snow is forecast for Friday night. If we get snowed in, we won't be able to!"

"Dad could come and get you in the Land Rover on Saturday morning," Mandy said at once.

"I could," agreed Dr. Adam. "But if the snow's really heavy, there might be drifting and the roads could be completely blocked. Maybe you should both go down to the village on Friday afternoon."

"And leave the dogs on their own? No," said Michael.

Hannah agreed. "My cousin Katie from Canada doesn't get here until Saturday morning, so there won't be anyone else to take care of the dogs until then."

Mandy stared at the thick white blanket that covered the fields. The moon was rising, full and bright. It cast a silvery sheen over the landscape, picking out the dark trail that the runners of the sled had carved out.

"Hold on!" Mandy said, an idea coming to her. "You've

got exactly what you need to get down to Welford in the snow."

"What's that?" asked Michael.

"An ace dogsled team!" Warming to her idea, Mandy went on, "It'll be a first for Welford, maybe for the whole of Yorkshire, a bride arriving for her wedding on a sled pulled by a team of huskies!"

"I love it!" said Hannah, her eyes shining. "And of course the dogs should be part of the wedding!"

"What about me?" asked Michael. "Do I get to go on the sled, too?"

"No. That's definitely not allowed." Mandy grinned. "The bride has to arrive on her own. But you could stay in town the night before so you'd only have to walk across from the inn on Saturday. And don't worry," she added quickly, as she guessed what Michael would say next, "I'll come up to the cottage on Friday afternoon to help Hannah. I can stay overnight and make sure she gets to the wedding on time!"

Late on Friday afternoon, just as more snowflakes started drifting down, Mandy and her dad arrived at Black Tor Cottage. Mandy had brought an overnight bag packed with her warmest clothes, plus the wedding present that her mom had finished wrapping for Hannah and Michael.

Quiver was sitting in the hall next to Michael's bags.

"Guarding the luggage?" Mandy asked Quiver, patting her.

"I think she's afraid we're abandoning her and the pups," said Hannah. "Suitcases and bags tend to upset her."

Mandy knelt down in front of Quiver. "Hannah and Michael would *never* abandon you," she said. "They love you so much they're bringing in a special person all the way from Canada to look after you while they're on their honeymoon."

Quiver thumped her tail on the floor as if to say she was happy with the arrangement.

"And James and I will come up to visit you," Mandy promised, which made Quiver wag her tail even faster.

After Dr. Adam and Michael had driven away, Mandy and Hannah went to settle the dogs in for the night. They were loose in the yard, stretching their legs before going to bed. When they saw Mandy and Hannah come out, they raced across to greet them.

"Whoa!" Mandy laughed as she was surrounded by a pack of excited huskies. Leo was among them, walking gingerly on his bandaged paw. "You look more cheerful than you did the other day," Mandy said, massaging his powerful shoulders.

"Time for bed," Hannah called, clapping her hands. "Some of you have a big day ahead of you."

"Especially you," Mandy said to Keira, who trotted alongside her. "You're going to be the best lead dog in the world tomorrow."

When Mandy awoke the next morning, she felt as if she and Hannah were completely cut off from the rest of the world. Deep, curling snowdrifts blocked the road, hiding the walls and hedges beneath sparkling white waves.

After breakfast, Mandy and Hannah let the dogs out before feeding them. As they raced around the yard, scattering snow from under their paws, Mandy gazed admiringly at the team that would be flying out to Anchorage. They were in superb condition, fit and powerful, their thick waterproof coats ready to withstand the harshest Alaskan weather.

"Which ones are going to pull the wedding sled?" Mandy asked Hannah.

"We'll stick to the same team we had yesterday," Hannah said. "Except for Dart. Just in case he decides to dart after a rabbit today! We'll put Alaska in his place."

When the dogs had stretched their legs, Hannah and Mandy rounded them up and took them back to their kennels for breakfast. As she took Keira's food into her pen, Mandy noticed a large red envelope sticking out of the wood paneling. She must have missed it in the dark last night.

TO HANNAH: DO NOT OPEN BEFORE SATURDAY, read the words on the front of the envelope. Puzzled, Mandy took it out to Hannah.

Hannah opened the envelope, frowning. Inside was a beautiful card with a red rose on the front. It was a Valentine's Day card from Michael!

"Of course!" Mandy exclaimed. "I forgot that it wasn't just your wedding day today!"

Hannah looked at her with a smile. "Do you think there's a card from a certain dog-loving young man waiting for you at home?" she teased.

Mandy felt herself go bright red. "No, I do not!" she said firmly. "James and I are just good friends!"

With the dogs fed, it was time for Hannah to get ready. While Hannah was in the bathroom, Mandy sat with Quiver and the puppies. They were two weeks old now, and were starting to play with one another. Nemo, the smallest by far at first, had caught up with his brothers and sisters and was a sturdy, adventurous little dog. Today he seemed determined to find a way out of the whelping box.

"Calm down," Mandy said as he scratched at the sides of the box. "I'm not sure that you're going to be a great leader one day. You're too independent!"

Nemo looked up at her with his startlingly blue eyes and grunted.

"But you know what?" Mandy chuckled, picking him up. "You'll always be my blue-eyed boy!"

When Hannah finally came out of the bathroom, Mandy gasped. This wasn't what she had been expecting at all! Apart from her long dark hair pinned up in pretty ringlets, Hannah didn't look remotely like a bride. Instead of a long white gown, she was wearing a ski suit and thick thermal socks.

"Are you ready?" Mandy said awkwardly.

Hannah laughed, reading her mind. "No. But I can't possibly wear my wedding gown on the sled. It's already at Animal Ark along with my bridesmaid's dress. I packed them in one of the bags your dad and Michael took with them last night."

Mandy grinned, suddenly realizing how absurd it would be for Hannah to steer the sled in her wedding dress.

They were just going out to prepare the sled when the phone rang. It was another of Hannah's cousins, whose thirteen-year-old daughter, Abigail, was going to be her bridesmaid. They were snowed-in on the other side of the mountains and wouldn't be able to make it to the wedding after all.

"That's too bad," Mandy said when Hannah told her the news. "Does that mean you're going to be missing a bridesmaid?"

"Not necessarily," Hannah smiled, and for a moment Mandy wondered if she was thinking of having Keira walk down the aisle behind her.

But Hannah had a different plan. "Would you do me another huge favor, Mandy?"

"I'll try."

"Besides being my assistant musher, would you be my bridesmaid? I'm sure the dress will fit you. And you deserve to wear it, because it's thanks to all your help that Michael and I have made it this far."

Mandy was so thrilled she could hardly speak. "Whoa!" she stammered. "I would be honored!"

"I can't think of anything else I'd rather be doing right now." Mandy sighed happily, sitting in the cargo bed and listening to the swish of the runners as the dogs pulled the sled down the hill to Welford.

"Me, neither," agreed Hannah from behind her. "Going to your wedding on a sled trimmed with white ribbons and swansdown beats everything else!"

Mandy glanced down at the bottom of the hill where the snow-covered roofs of Welford glistened in the sunshine. "Not long now," she said.

Forty minutes later, they pulled up outside Animal Ark. The snow in the lane was packed hard and not too deep, so it was an easy haul to the front door. Mandy's dad and mom came out to look after the dogs while Mandy and Hannah changed into their gowns.

As Hannah had predicted, the bridesmaid's dress could have been made for Mandy. It was a beautiful blue — the color of Keira's eyes — and when she walked downstairs, the long satin skirt swished around her legs, reminding her of the sound of the runners on the snow.

When the bride appeared, Mandy stared at her in delight. "You look fantastic! Like a princess from a fairy tale!"

Hannah smiled, her cheeks pink with excitement. She was wearing a beautiful, close-fitting dress trimmed in delicate lace. Over her shoulders, a cream-colored velvet cloak fell softly to the floor, stretching out behind her in an arc-shaped train.

There were flowers, too — a bouquet of perfect white roses for Hannah, and a nosegay of white daisies dotted with tiny blue flowers for Mandy. The florist had managed to deliver them to Animal Ark the previous day before the roads were closed.

Together, the bride and her bridesmaid went out onto the porch. "We're ready!" Mandy called to her dad.

"Well!" exclaimed Dr. Adam when he saw them. "What a transformation!"

"You look beautiful," Dr. Emily said to Hannah. You too, sweetie," she added, smiling at Mandy.

Dr. Adam looked at his watch. "I know you're supposed to be a few minutes late, Hannah, but you don't want Michael thinking you've had a mishap on the way down the hill. Why don't I drive you to the church now that the road's clear?"

Hannah looked horrified! "It's kind of you to offer," she said, "but no thanks. The only way I'm going to my wedding is on that sled. But with one change." She smiled at Mandy. "A bride never drives herself to the church. That means I'll have to sit in the cargo bed and you'll have to stand behind on the runners, Mandy, if you don't mind."

Mind! Mandy was thrilled. She just hoped she could remember all the tips she'd picked up from Simonie Nanogak, the owner of the dogsled tour company on Baffin Island. Then she met Keira's gaze, as the lead dog looked around at her from her position at the head of the team, and she knew she'd be fine.

"Hike up!" she called and gasped in delight as the

dogs trotted forward until their harnesses took up the slack, and the sled moved off with only a tiny jolt.

"You're doing great!" Hannah said quietly from the cargo bed. Mandy grinned, too busy concentrating on steering to reply.

The run to the church was straightforward because the road was flat and, even though there was less snow in the village than in the fields, there were no cars around. But there were plenty of pedestrians who stopped to watch the bridal sled go by. They cheered and waved, and Hannah waved back looking very regal.

Old Walter Pickard came out of the post office just as the sled swished past. "Well, I never!" he said. Mandy waved to him proudly.

Mrs. McFarlane, who ran the post office, came out, too. "How absolutely delightful!" she cried. She took a handkerchief out of the pocket of her overalls and dabbed her eyes.

The Reverend Hadcroft looked very startled when the sled pulled up in front of the church. "Goodness me," he said. "I've had horse-drawn carriages bringing the bride to the church before, but never a dog-drawn sled."

"This is no ordinary dogsled," Mandy told him, jumping off the runners as the sled eased to a halt. "You're looking at a winning team." She caught a glimpse of

Michael watching them from inside the church. She gave him a thumbs-up and he winked back.

Mandy looked around for somewhere to attach the snub line.

"I'll do that!" came an offer from the porch. It was James, looking pretty uncomfortable in a new gray suit. "I'm chief snub line operator, remember?" He grinned. Before he reached the sled, he stopped to take a photograph. "I don't think I'll ever see another wedding car like this one," he said.

With the snub line secured to a lamppost, Mandy helped Hannah out of the sled. She busied herself around Hannah, trying to remember everything she had to do as chief bridesmaid. She held the bouquet while Hannah climbed out of the sled, then straightened her dress, which was a little creased from being bunched up in the cramped cargo bed. Finally, she held up the bottom of the cloak to make sure it didn't get wet in the snow.

At last, they were ready to go in. A smiling, blond-haired man named Chad, who was Katie's husband, took Hannah's arm to lead her down the aisle. As they reached the door, a swell of organ music filled the air. It wasn't the usual bridal march Mandy had heard at other weddings, but something a lot more lively and dramatic. It reminded her of something. But what?

Hannah guessed what she was thinking. "Doesn't this music make you think of the dogs racing across the snow?" she whispered.

"Absolutely!" Mandy agreed. She could definitely hear dog paws tripping lightly over the snow in the music that surged around the church.

"It's a toccata by a composer named Widor. I can just imagine Keira in this part —" Hannah broke off. "Keira!" she said, and she spun around and ran back out of the church.

There was a loud gasp from the wedding guests, and Mandy saw Michael's face drop. It looked as if Hannah had changed her mind about getting married! But she stopped just outside, and crouched down beside Keira to whisper something to her.

Mandy saw the cloak start to slip off Hannah's shoulder. She dashed out to stop it from falling in the snow, and when she reached Hannah, she heard what she was saying.

"Thank you, darling Keira," the bride murmured. "If it weren't for you, we wouldn't be here today."

She stood up and shook out the creases in her dress. When she saw Mandy watching her anxiously, she smiled. "It's OK," she said. "I'm still getting married! I just needed to thank Keira. Whatever happens in the

Iditarod, I know that without her, I wouldn't be here today."

The organ music rang out more strongly now, like a team of huskies gathering themselves for an uphill run. Keira pricked her ears and put her head to one side to listen. Then she jumped up and licked Hannah, as if she were urging her to go to her new husband.

Mandy smiled. She knew she'd never meet another dog like Keira. The quiet, sensitive dog with a heart of gold had stepped in right when her owners had needed her, and made sure that Hannah and Michael's wedding was perfect! This truly was a Valentine's Day to remember.